1

D0498490

Rainbow Rainbow

Rainbow Rainbow

Stories

LYDIA CONKLIN

Catapult
New York

This is a work of fiction. All of the characters, organizations, and events portrayed in this collection of stories are either products of the author's imagination or are used fictitiously.

Copyright © 2022 by Lydia Conklin

All rights reserved

Grateful acknowledgment is made to the following publications for publishing the stories in their original form: "Laramie Time" in *American Short Fiction* and *Pushcart Prize 2020*; "The Black Winter of New England" in *The Gettysburg Review*; "Pioneer" in *The Southern Review* and *Mud City Review*; "Counselor of My Heart" in *The Southern Review*, *Pushcart Prize 2018*, and *Love Stories for Turbulent Times: Loving Through the Apocalypse* (Pushcart Press); "Sunny Talks" in *One Story*; "Ooh, the Suburbs" as "Rainbow Rainbow" in *The Paris Review*.

ISBN: 978-1-64622-101-1

Jacket design by Nicole Caputo
Book design by Wah-Ming Chang

Library of Congress Control Number: 2021947062

Catapult
New York, NY
books.catapult.co

Printed in the United States of America
1 3 5 7 9 10 8 6 4 2

For my parents—thank you for putting me into this weird world, and for everything that came after

Contents

Rainbow Rainbow

Laramie Time

MAGGIE AND I HAD BEEN LIVING IN WYOMING FOR three months when I finally agreed we could get pregnant. We were walking on a boulevard downtown over snow that was crunchy and slushy by turns, heading home from a disappointing lunch of lo mein made with white spaghetti. The air was so sharply freezing, the meal churning so unhappily through our guts, that I longed to cheer the afternoon. I'd made up my mind the week before, but I didn't find the right moment to tell her until we were trudging through uncleared drifts in front of the former movie theater. The Christian who'd bought the place for nothing had arranged the plastic letters into rhetoric on the marquee: GOD IS LISTENING GOD KNOWS YOURE ROTTEN.

"Maggie," I said, taking her hand. "I've decided." Last week's test results had exposed her declining fertility. If we wanted to do this, it had to be now.

She aimed her freckled stub nose at me and studied my face. "Where to get dessert?" She spoke bluntly, the joke of what she really hoped in the deadness of her words.

"I want to have a kid with you." I meant the words to

sound natural but invested with meaning—inflected emotion on *kid* and *you*—those two words the sum total of my future reality. But the sentence bumbled out, awkward, half-swallowed.

"Amazing." She spoke flatly, her unseasonable tennis shoes sinking into the slush. Why was she speaking flatly? Maggie had begged me for a kid for years. She should've jumped into my arms when I agreed. She should've fucked me right there on the boulevard, even though it was winter in Laramie, even though we're lesbians and fucking wouldn't help with getting the kid.

"Aren't you happy?"

A tear occluded one eye, but she squeezed it to a slit, squeezed both eyes closed. When she opened them, they were clear and dry. "Thank you. I am happy." She sounded mechanical. But sometimes she was like that—a sweet logic robot. She waited until we stepped onto the curb on Custer Street to clamp me in a cold hug.

That was it. After five years of debate. After crying and threatening to leave, after pointing out every child, even lumpy ones, after invoking hormones and decreased viability and geriatric pregnancies whenever worry or resentment surged through her. Not to mention last week's meltdown over the test results. And now look at her, unsurprised. Maybe she figured I wouldn't have moved across the country to spend a year deciding not to have a kid with her. But I was unpredictable and stubborn. She knew better than to count on me.

At thirty-seven, Maggie was three years older than me and beyond ready. I'd wanted to develop my career before motherhood—for the last few years I'd drawn a comic strip about lesbian turtles. Material success with comics seemed an impossibly distant goal, safe because it would take forever. No one bought the Sunday paper anymore and alt-weeklies were dead. And when would a comic strip about lesbian turtles ever hit the big time? Turtles are the least popular type of animal, and lesbians are the least popular type of human. But the strip launched briskly from a shabby online platform, with interest ballooning on social media. People fell in love with the painted turtle with her red dots by each ear and the bigger softshell turtle. People liked their warm, squinty eyes, I guess, their pointy overbites and the way they tried their best—flippers out, balanced on stubby flat feet—to press their plated chests together. The strip got syndicated in the surviving indie magazines and mainstream newspapers in cities like Portland and Portland. The pilot for a TV show had been funded and shot by a new, hip studio, which was considering buying a season. If the studio adopted the show, the turtles would appear on the small screen as black-and-white, stiff-moving cutouts, each character voiced by me, identically deadpan, and we'd move to LA. Whenever I remembered this possibility, I shuddered.

When the money for the pilot arrived, Maggie had asked to try. For years I'd given the excuse of my career—noble, logical, inarguable, and in the service, ultimately, of family. We needed money for a kid, of course, and Maggie didn't deserve a co-parent who was harried and drawing in the shadows, sneaking away from milestones to ink in shell plates and beaky mouths.

Once my career turned toward the light, I had to face my issues that were harder to articulate. My father claimed I'd cried when he first held me, and he took this as a permanent rejection of physical affection. He'd been clear that I was a compromise, that he didn't want kids. He demonstrated this, most days, by declining to participate. I was afraid my kid would feel the same—discarded, lonely. I'd never trust myself to be ready to welcome a little being to earth, though I was afraid to explain all this to Maggie, afraid she'd think I was loveless at my core. As months passed without my agreement, her frustrations accelerated.

Sometimes, when I was in a certain mood—a dangerous mood maybe, or cruel—I'd speculate on scenarios where the drudgery of domestic life provided me with a larger, more startling purpose, and I could almost justify making a child in my ambivalence. What if Maggie bore twins, one with my egg and one with hers? Our kids would bond so hard in the womb that it would be like me and Maggie combining in the popular, primal way. Maggie's pinched-nosed kid stroking her lips like Maggie did, smoothing her T-shirt like Maggie did, laughing in a high keen like Maggie did, falling in sibling love with my kid with dark messy hair and skinny wrists. Did sperm banks provide an anonymous grab-bag option? We could spend years gathering data on the father through the behavior of our child—he must have short eyebrows, he must like cantaloupe with pepper, he must be mean.

We'd moved to Wyoming at the end of the summer to "think about it" in a neutral zone while we survived off the rent from our subletted apartment in New York. We nicknamed this period the Laramie Time. Maggie had abandoned her career in academic publishing to finish a novel. Our best friend, Arun, a chatty professor, had lured us out west, making the forgotten town with its slouching wood-frame houses and white men who stared at anyone who was not a white man seem cool. He assured us cougars crossed the highway and food was cheap. He secured us free housing from his colleague on sabbatical.

Maggie had been straight until me, and the idea of Laramie bothered her less. But when I fretted over the move, Arun insisted that the famous hate crime had unfairly stigmatized the town. He watched me closely while he explained that every resident knew that Matt Shepard and his killer had been lovers. The crime wasn't homophobic or political but personal. As though that made it any easier to digest.

The colorful clouds and mountains, the antelopes and antelope-crushing brackets mounted to truck fenders, the beef, the clingy community of intellectual and creative semi-youths, they'd help the two of us decide one way or the other. And after three months of working side-by-side on the flower-patterned second-hand sofa, the tension of our future thickening the air and the results of Maggie's fertility test landing on us like rotten whipped cream to top it all, I'd come around to the idea of creating a tiny third party to cheer us up.

When Arun, our sole visitor, was with us, Maggie and I had fun, setting bobcat skulls on our scalps and dancing, playing the same cute girls as always. Those days were the best: Maggie suggesting the three of us drive numbered country roads to Bamforth or Curt Gowdy or Hot Springs, or wander the foothills seeking buffalo while she spun stories about cows with warnings encoded in their spots or swingers sleepwalking over the prairie. Time, for me, dissolved when she got that way, all joy: the pharmacy, the dentist, stopped traffic behind a horse. But when we were alone, she scowled into the tiles, gruff and unpleasant. When she managed to leave the apartment at all, she wandered Safeway, buying cans of beans and desiccated nubs of ginger, gazing with reproductive lust at any man. She'd given up on her novel. She was unemployed in a borrowed apartment in the middle of Wyoming. A kid, I hoped, could bring her back.

That evening, Maggie and I ate buttered tangles of pasta around a mushroom-shaped ironwork table that was intended for outdoor use. Snow spattered the windows. It was only November and already it had snowed so often that we didn't point it out anymore.

"So what should we name it?" I asked, to prove I was

serious. Maggie had always taken care of me—financially and otherwise. I owed her this baby. I popped open my hands. "Let's discuss."

She laughed in her snorting way that made my heart lift. Her hand found mine under the table. She squeezed my fingers over and over. "Are we doing Theme Day? All these noodles."

Back in New York, we used to sometimes focus all three meals on a color, or a texture, or some knobby vegetable pulled from the Chinatown market. I stroked her fingers so she'd relax her mechanical squeezing. Her hand seized up.

"I'm serious," I said. "About the names. You must've thought of ideas."

"You're getting ahead of yourself," she said. "It's not even conceived."

I shrugged. "But it's fun to talk about, right?"

"Jane," she said, anchoring her straw-colored hair behind her ear. "Or Michael. I'm sick of all those pretentious names."

She returned to her pasta—the subject over, decided. What else would we talk about for however long it took to conceive plus *nine months*? Wasn't jabbering about baby names, flapping through giant volumes, revisiting the hi-jinks of relatives long dead, how a couple worked up excitement over a forthcoming wrinkled intruder? What about Francine? What about Jiminy? What about Puck?

Maybe she'd reacted so glumly because of the lesbian turtles. Three weeks before, they'd agreed to adopt a gerbil with much more fanfare than I'd offered her. They'd cried.

They'd crinkled their papery skin and performed their shell-slapping embrace.

The next morning, I found Maggie pouring coffee to fuel her standard day of calling friends, useless shopping, walks that went nowhere, window sessions watching fake cowboys saunter by. She freelanced, but that only filled a few hours a week, which she stretched out by typing extra slowly.

"I better finish my work," she said, a bite in her voice already. "Wouldn't want to disappoint all the clamoring souls who rely on me." She splashed coffee into her bowl until it spilled over.

Maggie admitted to thinking about her novel sometimes while she lazed around, though she maintained that she'd given up, that there was no point pouring your life into some document no one would ever read. What worried me was how she discussed the project of art: miserable, challenging, like she wanted me to quit my comic and mope around with her. I refused to get sucked into hopelessness. My grip on my work was shaky enough.

I snagged Maggie's sleeve as she passed.

"Watch out." She brushed my hand away to protect her coffee. She looked like a mole, like she always did at this hour, which was sweet. But today she looked worse than usual. The skin at the corners of her eyes was blue, and her cheeks were rough-textured the way they got when she was stressed. I'd hoped my agreement would make her happy.

The turtles had hosted a garden party to celebrate their choice, frogs and tortoises emerging from under lily pads to fete the future moms.

Maggie jiggled her coffee bowl. "Can I sit, please? Am I allowed?"

"Here." I pushed away my sketches. She scowled.

Most mornings I headed straight to my brush and dish of ink. Lately I had conference calls too, and sometimes I was in LA. I had treatments to rewrite and producers to please and animators to supervise. Half of what I did for the show—which the producers had dumbed down to *Bisexual Turtles*—I did in a trance. Whenever Maggie asked about moving to LA, wringing her hands and fretting about highways and smog and glad-handers talking shop, I told her not to worry. She was such a New York girl, striding through Manhattan in her black coat, snapping her way through editorial meetings while clinging to paper cups of coffee, acquiring her first-choice titles, always. Laramie was a way station, but LA was permanent, and the enemy.

I'd take my commitment one step further by discussing the sperm donor. The turtles only had to visit Gerbil-O-Rama—the shop that appeared on their shore the moment they needed it. We, on the other hand, had a process to slog through. Why not start? Maggie had abandoned her career and writing and left herself with nothing. Maybe she wanted a kid to distract herself from losing her novel. That was fair. I wanted that for her too.

I laced my fingers. "So," I said. "The journey begins."

She took a sip of coffee, squinting through the steam. "Excuse me?"

"So," I said. "The journey begins."

She set her bowl down. "I heard you. I just don't have any idea what you're talking about."

Had she forgotten what we'd decided? "Our journey to have a child."

Brightness flamed over her face, then extinguished. "What did you want to discuss?"

"We decided to do it," I reviewed. "We settled on names. What's left?"

"To get pregnant and have a baby and raise it to adulthood." She spared a smile for her own joke. "If something's on your mind, just say it." One eye checked me curiously.

"The *sperm*," I said proudly.

"Jesus, Leigh." She peered at me up and down. "You're really jumping in, aren't you? You're really on honor roll all of a sudden."

"We have to select a man who embodies our values and love. We could have a fun ceremony where friends help choose from the sperm bank." We'd be leagues more thorough than the turtles, who'd simply reached for the cutest gerbil in the box. We'd invite our Laramie acquaintances to debate dad options. I'd brandish placards with photographs of males and statistics. Did we want a San Francisco engineer who's Boastful, Fun, and Curious? Or a math teacher who's Creative, Wry, and Caring? Did we want a soccer buff who enjoys Potatoes, Chats, and Items? Or an oak tree fan with a

Meaningful Childhood I Long to Replicate in a Baby Version of Myself?

"But Arun," she said, studying me.

"What?"

"Who else?" The top of her face shone with anticipation, while her mouth remained downturned.

"Are you okay?" I inched my chair closer. I longed to embrace her, but she looked prickly.

"I'm fine." She kissed me, sending a leak of molasses from my mouth to my core. If we weren't discussing such urgent matters, if she wasn't in a rotten mood, I'd have invited her upstairs to hide with me in the covers.

"Are you sure?"

"Certainly," she said, in her professional voice, her hand sliding off my shoulder. "You've thought about it, haven't you?"

But, of course, Arun was better than anyone narcissistic or desperate enough to peddle their bodily fluids. He was handsome and brilliant, an innovative critic whose mission was to write accessibly and increase public access to literary analysis. And he was our best friend. We'd known him since he was a graduate student in New York. We had endless fun in our group of three, while both of us were also close with him on our own. Still, I was disappointed not to debate. "He's a start. But wouldn't it be fun to throw around options?" I was desperate to discuss the decision, to comb through details, to convince myself this was real. Her vagueness, her rush to wrap up, was disturbing. "What about Rudyard?"

"Rudyard Beechpole? With the lank hair and aging rock-star face?"

"He makes great chairs." His chairs were carved from blackwood with curlicues whittled into the seats like worm-holes. We'd wanted one until we'd seen the price.

"I don't care if my baby makes chairs," Maggie said.

"I wouldn't *mind* new chairs." I envisioned the apartment filling with increasingly elegant furniture as our baby developed as a craftsman.

Maggie snorted. "So Beechpole is a contender for you?"

"Not really." I said, confused. Arun *was* the perfect donor. And I loved the names Michael and Jane. "I'll call Arun now."

Maggie looked up with a surprised frown. "Are you sure?"

I laid my hands flat on the table. "Maggie. Seriously. What's up with you?"

"I was just asking." Her coffee was nearly gone. She turned her bowl, swirling the dregs.

"I thought you wanted kids? I thought that was the central theme of our relationship?"

Her voice quieted. "But I want to know what you think."

"I said I want to do this. I'm discussing the particulars." I pressed down until my hands patterned with the table's texture. "What more do you want?"

Maggie watched me, eyes pleading. I was terrified to question her further, afraid to unearth what was going through her mind. She got up and turned into the sink, rinsing her bowl for ages after it was clean. Had she only wanted babies so intensely due to my resistance? I watched her until she looked away.

For the rest of the day, I sketched Maggie in turtle form, finally appreciating my willingness to have a kid: kissing me with her beak, stroking me with her flat foot, dedicating to me the most intricate plate of her shell.

The weather turned the next week. Instead of dry slate skies confettied with snow, we were icy and windy and colder than ever. The hail gunfired down, cutting at the glass, and even the cowboys stayed inside. We ate canned corn with flaccid carrots on the days we couldn't bear to trudge to the convenience store and treat ourselves to sad packets of gummy fish and crumbly Wyoming pork rinds.

Arun burst apart with happiness before I got the words out, gushing that he'd never wanted to raise his own kids, so he'd hoped we'd ask. On my own, I arranged and paid for his genetic and STI tests and hired a lawyer to draft a contract forfeiting his parental rights. We added a clause that we'd welcome informal involvement as all parties saw fit.

I wasn't ready for the kid itself, but each step toward the kid was manageable. I consulted with the doctor over Arun's perfect genetic score, initialing the contract, cutting checks from my turtle earnings. I was giving someone I loved what she wanted, though Maggie remained tepid, greenlighting each step without engaging. I acclimated to her coolness on the subject. Though it worried me in spikes, she'd waded through troughs of depression before. And maybe nothing was exciting when you'd wanted it too long. Maybe she'd burned out getting us to here. When the baby came, surely she'd revive.

I bought her the thermometer and predictor sticks and vitamins and a logbook, and though she showed no initiative, she used them at my urging, maintaining a record by the bed. She didn't tell me when her body was ready. But I checked her journal, and when her LH hormone surged, I announced I was calling Arun.

I couldn't wait to see him. Arun was sparkly. He would've been a star anywhere. He listened closely, as though what you said mattered, he was goofy the way men never are—subjugating himself for a laugh—and he was beautiful: his hair a soft ripple, his cheeks padded with the flesh of a teen. Once he was back in the apartment, the whole endeavor would make sense again.

Our first two months in Laramie, we saw Arun daily. He worked next to us on the couch after his classes and ate with us at the nineties-style vegetarian restaurant that leaned too heavily on bulgur. We hiked on the weekends without finding trails or paying for parks. We picked any mountain and pulled over on the country highway and marched through sagebrush and over deer ribs until we achieved the top, Maggie clinging to my arm, leaning her cheek against my shoulder and infusing me with love. She gathered treasures: a whistle, a lizard head, a thorn as thick as a fang. I saved them all.

One afternoon, at the summit of our favorite mountain,

all of Laramie squatted before us. While Maggie exclaimed over the prairie, I pictured Matthew Shepard out there on a fence, slowly dying. Maggie asked what I was thinking and I said nothing; it was all so beautiful.

"I'm cold," Arun said, and Maggie threw him her tank top as a joke, spinning off like a naked animal into the aspens. He pried the shirt over his head. The straps stretched across the drum of his chest, the cotton nearly tearing, and he called Maggie back, opening his arms. "Look—I'm finally a lesbian." We laughed until we crashed down into the chaparral. That was the last afternoon Maggie and I were easy with each other.

The day after her positive surge, I met Arun at the door to our apartment building, by the block glass in the stairwell. His hand trembled as he brushed ice off his shoulder. "Am I early?"

"You're perfect." I sounded like I was hissing, "*Let me steal your genes.*"

"Cool," Arun said. "I guess I should come in?"

I led him to the living room. Maggie was waiting upstairs. She was too nervous to socialize until the process was complete, but it felt wrong to send Arun off to masturbate instantly. Besides, I liked his company. Here was this thirty-five-year-old man, beautiful and brilliant with a perfect job, fine without a baby or even a girlfriend. He saw a few girls in town and sometimes took trips to LA, returning sunny and fortified. But largely he was the picture of someone who could be happy alone.

"How's my Maggie?" he asked.

"She's great." Arun loved Maggie best. Everyone did. She was pretty, like a fairytale girl lost in the woods, but brilliant. Everyone said she should go for a PhD before she got too old. "She's waiting upstairs."

"I forgot what she looks like, it's been so long." He scratched the stiff chin of the taxidermied prairie dog we'd all bought on a joyride to Centennial. "If it weren't for the paperwork, I wouldn't have seen you either."

"Things have been rough."

He looked up, eyes big. "Oh, I know."

"Can I get you a drink?"

"Nice seduction technique," he said. "It's 2:00 p.m."

"How about pork rinds?"

"I'll take a drink. By the way, this is the weirdest thing I've ever done."

I'd been headed to the kitchen and I turned to laugh— Arun always put me at ease, how had I forgotten—but his face, forever photo-ready, had collapsed.

"You okay?"

"Just get me a drink." His tone was steely.

In the kitchen, I fretted over what to serve. I'd stocked his favorites—beer, Jack and Coke, single-serving cans of a spritzer called Naughty Fruits—but none felt tonally appropriate. I pulled down a bottle of tangerine Schnapps, left over from a Christmas pudding, some bitters, and a novelty soda called Cool Mint Surprise. I whipped these with egg whites, grape jelly, and coconut shavings. The colors refused to integrate, though, and the drink was a bubbling, breathing rainbow.

Arun took one confused peek at my creation, helped himself to a swig, and grimaced. I wanted to tell him the drink was supposed to be funny. When he swallowed, liquid bulged down his throat. His face squished like he might throw up.

"Listen," I said. "You don't have to do this."

Arun gulped more rainbow. Egg white foamed on his chin. "You know I want to." He threw back another sip and the green layer of the drink splashed his shirt. He didn't seem to notice.

"Are you worried you won't get off or something?"

He nodded slowly. "I don't masturbate that often."

I held my face steady. "You don't?"

"I'm sure I'll squeeze one out."

"Great." In my comic, Arun was a lanky, long-legged tortoise named AJ who stopped by with sour-cream and-onion snails and reptile puns. As a Shakespeare scholar, Arun found my comic unforgivably bizarre, though he treasured the small fame it afforded him with queer hipsters on campus. He'd been the most popular character since the beginning, according to the Twitterverse. *If AJ isn't on the show, I'll slit my wrist with a box cutter*, a tween had typed.

"You guys are good?" he asked, shifting his focus to the ceiling.

"Of course." Since we'd moved to Laramie, I'd never seen Arun alone. "What do you mean?"

He shrugged at the ink on my wrist. I hadn't slept, so I'd drawn all night. "Your career."

This startled me. The issue with Maggie had always been kids. Everything else was perfect—the sex, the conversation; we both loved hiking and rice and audiobooks and begging bakeries for fresh bread at 4:00 a.m. Neither of us cleaned refrigerators or harped on dusting. The lesbian turtles had the same sole problem. In one strip, they gazed into each other's beady eyes and whispered that they wished baby turtles didn't exist, that eggs couldn't gel in their ovaries, or that reproduction was automatic or mandatory, so no decision was necessary. "There's just that one issue between Maggie and me," I'd told friends. "That one hitch."

Arun relaxed against the cushions. "I mean, think about it. Your comic goes viral, it's bought by some hip feminist studio, you might get a bigshot writing gig in LA?"

"She's supportive."

"No kidding." Arun leaned forward, elbows on knees. "But think about it, Leigh. What's Maggie doing?"

"Right now? Waiting." I dropped stiffly into a chair. With no one to confide in, I hadn't faced a hard truth in months.

"No, honey. She quit her job. She's editing, like, ten pages a week for some startup."

"But that's her choice." That last night of Maggie's novel, she'd typed feverishly since predawn. She'd requested a stay on dinner, then another. As bedtime approached and we still hadn't eaten, she shoved her laptop off the couch. "It's all made up." Her fingers fluttered on the air. "Completely fake." Panic flickered in her eyes, but her body sagged in relief. Maggie's novel was a drug. She'd worked on it constantly, miserably. She was a great writer—this was obvious even from her goofy road trip yarns—but writing made her miserable.

Arun watched me. "Do you really believe she'd give up?"

"It was sad, yeah, but she said she wanted it." Guilt tugged at me. I suppose I should've tried to change her mind. I'd been too relieved to have my girlfriend back.

"Meanwhile, teen girls are coming over your turtles on Snapchat. And she's doing nothing. You really believe that?"

I should've worked through the abandonment of her novel, ascertained Maggie was all right. I should've offered to read her book, or at least assured her I believed in her. We hadn't talked about ourselves in ages. The kid question had subsumed us. If we discussed her novel, or LA, we circled back to kids. But I understood, with Arun's disapproving gaze settling over me, that I should've forced the issue.

"That's why this is good." I gestured at Arun, accidentally aiming at his groin. We both grimaced. "Really, though. I've done what I wanted to do. And now I can do this." Instead of *this* I almost said *what Maggie wants to do.*

Arun shook his head. "I should shut up." His face softened like it would at a child. "But she's still working on her novel, Leigh. She has been all this time."

My body tightened. "What do you mean."

"It's going well," he whispered. "Really well. So you don't have to worry." He leaned back and nodded, as though waiting for me to leap from my chair and dance.

"Oh." My mouth stayed frozen. Maggie had been lying? Sneaking off to write? When? While I was asleep? When she was pretending to freelance? When I was in LA? I saw her waking at four after I left for a business trip, indulging in fifteen hours of writing, twenty, forsaking meals and snacks and the bathroom, her eyes burning dry, thrilled and alive. I'd understand if the work was going badly, if she wanted to turn the corner before she shared the news. But Maggie couldn't write around me, couldn't celebrate. Because of the turtles, or something else. "I knew that."

Arun raised his eyebrows. "Did you?"

"Of course she told me. And I would've noticed anyway. You think she could hide that?" The words sent a crack of pain down my neck. We'd drifted so far apart. I'd failed to recognize creative euphoria in my own partner, living beside me in the middle of nowhere for three months. What was wrong with me? I cleared my throat, trying to sound natural: "Can I ask you something?"

Arun nodded, watching with concern.

"Why don't you want to raise kids?"

Egg white shone opalescent on his chin. "You want to know?"

"Of course." Nothing he'd say would change my mind. I'd heard all the arguments. I'd made them myself—global health, overpopulation, climate change, career surrender, drudgery. I hated chores. I hated shopping. I only liked one in a hundred kids—those were tricky odds. I didn't want kiddie barfing diseases. I didn't care about advancing my genes.

I didn't want Maggie's body to change. I didn't want to read a book about parenting. But everyone said once the kid was born, you were happy.

"No one would admit they made a mistake," he said. "By having a kid, I mean. There's too much investment."

"Yeah, yeah." I'd thought of that.

"That's not why I'm scared, though."

I should've ended the conversation—Maggie was waiting—but I had to ask. "Then why?"

"My nephew," he said, "lives in Queens. When he was four he escaped his bed. He opened the front door and stood outside until a bus stopped. He got on the bus and rode into Manhattan."

"No." Arun exaggerated all the time for laughs.

"He did." Arun set his empty glass on our steamer trunk. "My brother and his wife were asleep. They think the bus driver was high, but I bet everyone thought Sunil was with someone else. He rode over the Queensboro Bridge and into Midtown. He got off at Lincoln Center. Seriously." Arun wore that hurt look he got when he feared we didn't believe him. "Later people said they wondered about the kid. But no one did anything." He rolled his eyes. "New Yorkers, man. No offense."

Arun had forsaken New York to live as a pure Westerner. "Hey," I said. "I'm in Wyoming now." If I'd found that kid I would've scooped him up and ferried him to safety. I would've made him laugh in my arms until his parents claimed him.

"Anyway," Arun said. "This lady found him."

"Phew," I said.

"No." His face darkened. "It's not good."

Arun never talked about his family. His parents were nasty to him and, I suspected, abusive. Part of his love for Laramie was that there were only two planes a day into town. You saw one dangling in the sky and knew your visitor was on board. No one could sneak up on you out here.

"They went to a play." Arun frowned. "I guess it had some weird stuff. A man dressed as a wolf, some naked kid, a stone people handled. It was a festival entry—the script isn't published. I've checked. I'm sure you would've loved it."

"So they saw a play," I said. "So?" I liked the idea of a kid at a play: head bobbing at knee level, following me to museums and parks and afternoon pubs. Having a kid didn't mean we were doomed to languish in pits of plastic balls.

"And we could figure out what he saw, right? We could find the script, interview audience members. But what gets me is the time around the play. Like what kind of person—and not to be sexist, but what kind of woman—sees a four-year-old lost in Midtown Manhattan and doesn't call the police? Instead she takes him to a goddamn play."

I looked at the ceiling. Maggie must be angry we were taking so long. Stress impaired conception. I pictured the wrinkles around her mouth deepening. I was afraid to face her, afraid of the girl who'd lied about her brilliant novel.

"Something bad happened. Sunil wasn't the same after. He turned into this mini-adult. He didn't bounce around like he used to. You don't understand—he was a puppy before. These questions and silly voices all the time—even in timeouts he'd dance in his corner—and then, nothing. And it wasn't just the play. He didn't understand the play."

"You think she molested him?" My heart skipped. I hadn't met Sunil, but I pictured him anxiously eager, little hands grabbing the air, clowning as he bounced from foot to foot.

"We'll never know." A moody expression bled over Arun. "Because he doesn't know, but it affected him. He can't tell us. Did she touch him? Did she say something? Did she show him a picture?" He gripped his knee. "Whenever I think of having kids, I fall into that panic. I know it would never happen again, but a thousand situations like it would. Little moments, sure, but I can't stand the idea of letting the kid loose to live a private life." He shook his head. "That spooks me."

"I get it," I said.

"I shouldn't say this crap to you." He raised his tumbler. "Your rainbow juice made me do it."

I lifted my water, and we clicked glasses.

"But it's okay—you're not paranoid," he said. "You haven't had my family." He didn't know about my father, how I'd been unwanted. My story was pathetic in the face of the darkness he'd just shared.

"You'll be a beautiful mother," he said, regret wet in his eyes, whether for his own childhood or his missed fatherhood, I couldn't tell.

I had a flash of wishing I'd been Arun's mother. No, Sunil's. I saw a hairy, upright beast lurching across the stage, a boy too shy to seize the sleeve of his chaperone. When it came down to assuming responsibility for a floppy body, loose in the world, I was sure I could be flexible and resilient, that I could put a little person first. Not only that I could do it but that I wanted to, and not only that I wanted to but that I had to.

I sent Arun upstairs with my laptop and a glass vial. I should've checked on Maggie, but the news about her novel, and Arun's story, had me jittery. I lingered between my office, where Arun produced the ingredient, and our bedroom, where Maggie lay. Both rooms radiated tense silence.

I could picture my child, finally: small and dark-haired, strolling with me at the foot of the mountains. She was real to me now, so real I was afraid to touch the air at my hip for fear of grazing her head. But when I pictured life with her, Maggie wasn't with us. I saw myself and the child, or the child alone, or another figure between us. Arun, even, but not Maggie. I'd told myself our relationship was perfect, and I hadn't worried enough when the freeze set in. But she was writing away in secret, while pretending to be depressed—or she really was depressed. Maybe the novel was going well and she was sad she couldn't share that—because of my success, or because of competition between us, or maybe the novel was about us and she didn't want me to know. Whatever the reason, we couldn't survive like this.

Losing both her and that dark-haired kid was a double punch in the gut. I loved Maggie. And I loved the kid already so much, ridiculously much, and she'd never even breathe. Now I understood what I'd lost: a girlfriend and a little person in a jasmine-flavored yard in Los Feliz, pulling vines off the house and training them up jacaranda trees, drawing with a sleeping baby's sunlit face pointing up at me from a cozy sling. The hot red loops of nostrils, the mouth sealed with no reason to ever cry, the smell of sweet bread rising from that golden scalp.

I braced myself to tell her. But then I put it together. After I'd agreed to have kids, Maggie had never raised the issue once. She didn't want a baby, or she'd come to the same conclusion I had and was afraid to tell me. So maybe we were on the same page. Maybe we could be okay.

The door to the office opened. One of Arun's hands protected his crotch while the other extended the vial.

"Don't look at it," he said. "That's too weird."

"Thanks," I said. "You can go."

He looked at me, wounded. "Just like that?"

"I'm sorry." I wanted this whole sad attempt over. "Please, Arun."

"Okay, fine." He'd hoped to be part of the family maybe, though he'd signed his rights away. "So long as you aren't mad. About my story or whatever."

Of course I was mad. "I'll call you."

I held the vial with two hands as Arun thumped down the stairs. The plan had been to keep the fluid warm and draw it with the syringe. I opened the bedroom door with a shaking hand.

Maggie was stretched naked on the bedspread. Her tawny hair covered her shoulders and the tops of her breasts. She smelled like sun-soaked hay: dry and hot and safe. This person had lied to me. She was happier than she could admit; she was thriving. My heart lifted for her joy, even if it was separate from me.

"Hi," she whispered.

Warmth filled me despite the underheated room. I hadn't encountered Maggie like this—lips melting, skin relaxed and smooth, breasts flushed pink—in weeks. I'd forgotten her body ready for me. "You okay?" I whispered.

"Can't you tell?"

She lifted her arms and I dropped into them, the vial still clutched in my fist, heating it with all my might. Maggie's velvet skin was exactly right, her skinny limbs curving around me, the ache of her breath on my forehead. "What changed?" I asked.

She pulled her head back. She was glowing. "I had to know you're serious."

The vial cooled between my fingers. How had this sludge been so recently inside a body? She wanted a baby.

"You were testing me?" I flashed with fuzzy, distant rage.

She tipped her head back. "Don't talk. Just touch me."

I was so grateful to be back with her that, even as a barb of anxiety drew through me, I hung above her, our bellies grazing. I saw Sunil in the dark as a man-wolf stalked the stage, seeking someone familiar. The turtles' gerbil, so sweet and easy that he could never exist. He might be the only baby I'd ever create. But I couldn't do it with Maggie. Not the silence and manipulation and lies. Not with a kid.

Tomorrow I'd tell her what I was about to do. We'd fight, in a subdued, broken way, and we'd be over. The enormity of what I'd done wouldn't hit her for days, when she'd call me, furious. I'd leave her without a job or a girlfriend or a kid. I already knew how our end would play out, and I'd be right.

I drew the semen into the syringe. But before I pushed it into Maggie I aimed the tip down and pressed the plunger, freeing the sperm under the bed. Our baby, soaking into the carpet, my only chance, as it would turn out, and hers too. A shudder shook through me. I dipped the syringe into her and then I lay on her body, focusing on her dusty mammal smell.

The Black Winter of New England

HAZEL LEARNS ABOUT THE NEW YEAR'S PARTY WHILE in the graveyard behind Sacred Heart. Melissa and Kit crouch downhill from her and explain. Since Hazel is sitting higher than them, she can see the sky; the clouds press together in an upside-down bowl. Black trees ring the bowl at the horizon, more like tree holes, really, where trees fell through and left a mark. The cherry sun teeters just above. Soon it will suck down into the branches, and the evening will be dark and freezing. Melissa and Kit are underdressed, but Hazel has mittens and snow pants strapped up around a flannel shirt.

"I don't get it," Hazel says.

"What's not to get?" Melissa says, shaking hair over her shoulder. "We go to her house at ten and party. There's gonna be high school boys."

"But how can I go out at ten?" Hazel asks. "My curfew's eight thirty."

"Your parents are sixty," Kit says. "They go to bed at nine."

"They're technically fifty-four." Hazel scratches the number into a patch of dirt with a twig. Her parents are old, yeah, but not sixty. So what if they go to bed at nine? Hazel does too. Sometimes, before she goes to sleep, she takes her pet rat into bed and lets it run over her, its nails pulling up loops of thread on the comforter. "Whose house is it again?"

"Esther Meng's," says Melissa. "Jesus, do we have to write it down?"

"I'm not certain I'll remember the date, is all."

"It's *New Year's Eve*," says Melissa, kicking snow that survived the last melting massacre. The powder scatters into nothing when her sneaker strikes.

Melissa and Kit have been Hazel's friends for all of seventh grade, and she thinks about them each minute. Before this year Hazel stuck close to home, but now she has trouble sitting still, even in school. The world is so much sharper now. And when she's with Melissa and Kit, it's sharpest of all. She never knows what to expect when she marches with them down the Diamond Middle School driveway, into the afternoon air. Each day is its own adventure. Sometimes they switch outfits, including underwear, in the hair-care aisle of CVS. Other times they drop grapes off the bridge above the interstate, simulating a plague of eyeballs. Lately, though, Melissa and Kit have been going over to this Esther Meng person's house, whoever that is.

Melissa squints at Hazel, setting her jaw in the way that means she's about to pronounce judgment, and Hazel's cells shrink. When Melissa loves Hazel, all is right, but she can be mean. She calls Kit a pervert for being a lesbian, and when Hazel didn't know what a donkey punch was, Melissa spat on her shoe.

"Sometimes I don't know if you're dumb or just crazy," Melissa says now. "But I know you're not dumb."

"I'm not crazy," Hazel says, though sometimes her thoughts jitter in a certain way, like molecules moving in the night.

"Chill out, everybody," Kit says. "Let's do a practice sex and then go home."

Maybe Melissa will practice on Hazel. The notion jars her, but she wilts when, once again, Melissa takes Kit's shoulder in that irresistible, tender way, the way she never touches anyone outside the practices. "Are you ready?" Melissa's voice is hard and low.

Kit lies down on the slope, on her back like the corpses buried under her. Hazel wipes her hands off on her snow pants and pins Kit's wrists into the icy grass, tight enough to cut the dirt. She must hold Kit in place while Melissa dips her fingers into Kit's body. Not that Kit would try to escape.

The air shivers. Melissa unzips Kit's jeans and slips them to her knees. This is Hazel's favorite time, when anything in the world could happen. This is the moment when she most clearly understands that she would do anything for Melissa.

Kit closes her shivering thighs. "Put me out of my misery." She squints at the fading sky. She always falls silent at this stage, as though she's entering a fresh land, her mouth displaying a narrow strip of teeth. Melissa hooks a finger into the elastic of Kit's underwear and pulls down. A puff of hair springs out.

"You gotta shave, man," says Melissa. "At least before New Year's."

Kit shakes her head. "You can't cut it while it's still growing."

Kit has the most body hair of the three girls, but her head is buzzed. In the cold, her scalp is red between the follicles. Hazel wants to give her a hat but can't disturb the moment, everything hanging on thick rubber air.

Melissa releases Kit's underwear, the elastic snapping up, and leans back. Hazel clings to Kit's wrists. They can't stop now. They need this for the friendship.

"I don't have the heart for this today," Melissa says. "I can't stop thinking about New Year's." She stands up against the sky, glowing in the evening as though she's been painted with bright oils. Even though her body could belong to a boy their age, skinny and flat under her Korn hoodie and ballooning jeans, her hair is long and yellow, cropped straight without bangs or layers, parted in the center and bending glossily around her skull. Her foxy muzzle tips up, the pimples on her chin full and angry.

She looks hungrier than ever, her gaze aimed above Kit's half-dressed body and into the snow-fat clouds, like she wants to rip free and disappear, a dog racing into the woods. She's going to leave. Hazel wants to grab her and make her stay, but her attention is already destroyed. Melissa crosses the parking lot back to her mom's duplex. She jumps on all the leftover snow, erasing it into gray powder.

Kit pulls her jeans up over purpling thighs, scrapes slush from her shoe on the edge of a headstone.

"I guess we better head out too." Kit kicks a puffy marble grave. "It's late."

It feels late, but it's not, really. Melissa shouldn't have left. Though it's dark, it's only five. The black winter of New England, Hazel's father calls it. And he's just inside all day. He doesn't have to face it. In August, when the air was thick and damp, the president spoke on TV of a girl with wild hair and an angry smile, a girl he'd almost had sex with, but instead they'd done weirder things. People discuss the details with heavy tones: dresses, stains, private meetings Hazel didn't understand, and it's too late now to ask.

"The party's going to be epic." Kit rubs her skull. "Really, Hazel, you should go. We keep meeting people and telling them about you and they're like, 'Who is this chick? Does she even exist?'"

Hazel pictures herself at the edge of a group of people she never knew lived in Lexington, wedging herself into the fold as they danced and bit and frolicked. "My parents probably won't let me."

"We already *talked* about this. You're not *telling* them, remember? Jesus. Don't let Melissa hear you say that. She'll feed you to your rat."

Hazel hates the idea of her parents thinking she's in bed when she's somewhere across town at the mercy of kids she's never met.

"I think I'll ask them." She touches the corner of her lip, which is starting to freeze over.

When Hazel gets home she checks the calendar of national and state parks in the kitchen. They're up to Glacier National Park in Montana, which looks tropical compared to Lexington. A rainbow bridges two folded fabric peaks. A billy goat in the foreground laughs, gape-mouthed with Easter bunny ears.

New Year's Eve is two days away, on Thursday. She feels like just yesterday her family was exchanging trinkets on Christmas Eve in Syracuse amid a herd of cousins too young to have any interest in Hazel. But now they're back already, having left on Christmas to beat traffic. Now it's 1999 in two days. And then just one more year until the whole millennium's over.

Hazel enters the living room. Across the Oriental rug, her parents are in their matching toile armchairs like they always are when they're not at work. Her father is reading a mystery, and her mother is reading the mystery her father read last week. Her father is always one book ahead. He's always saying stuff like, "Did you get to the tuning fork in the gullet yet?"

Sometimes Hazel wonders when her father read that

first book. Maybe someone read it to him before her mom was born, because he's six months older. Maybe they haven't always read mysteries. Maybe, before Hazel was born, they read westerns. Maybe, when she goes to college, they'll read science fiction. Hazel's dad will zoom ahead by light-years instead of pages. He'll maul mutants on Uranus while Hazel's mother stays on Earth, looking at the sky. If he gives away the end, she won't even understand the language.

On the way to her parents and their mysteries stands a gauntlet of collections in curio cabinets and lightfast boxes. Hazel's father is a big collector. He collects marbles and bookends and custard cups. He collects hatpins too, but he says Hazel's mom collects them. "Show them your pins," he says when visitors come. Hazel's mom offers the cushion stuck through with baby silver arrows, but Hazel's dad does the talking. He shows which pins were handmade before the switch to mass production in 1832, which models were outlawed due to dangerous length. Sometimes he aims an illegal one at a guest's eye, laughing like a crazy person. That's supposed to be a joke. Hazel used to be embarrassed by the collections, didn't invite friends over because of them, but Melissa and Kit trot past the living room without a glance.

"Mom and Dad," Hazel says, pressing her toes into the border of the rug. "I have a question."

"Take off your snow pants," her dad says. "You're inside."

"Let me ask first." She has to get the question out before they lecture her, if she's to have any chance. And she does want to go to the party, she's pretty sure. Even if it's scary.

"You're slushing all over the carpet in here. Jesus Christ."

Hazel swallows the back talk welling in her throat. She has to stay on her father's good side. She treks to the foyer and unbuckles her snow pants. She throws them on the newel post, where they land on coats and scarves piled like a mass of colorful ice cream. When she returns to the living room her mom rises for tea.

"Do you want lemon ginger, Haze?"

"No, but let me ask first."

"Go ahead," her father says. "No one's stopping you."

"I just wanted to ask. Like, there's this party."

"A birthday party?"

"For New Year's."

"Well, I didn't see a card for that." Hazel's father shifts in his chair, making a sound like farting.

"Melissa and Kit invited me in person."

Hazel's dad shakes his head. He says Melissa's eyes are clotted with makeup and that kids with single moms go feral. Once Melissa's mom came to pick Melissa up, and he didn't show her the pins. He wedged his body in the door, sealing the house until Melissa came down to leave. "That sounds like it goes past eight thirty."

"That's the whole point." He won't understand if Hazel says she wants to know what Esther Meng is like, or that she can't stand to be parted from Melissa and Kit for yet another defining episode. "I want to see the new year start."

"Those parties aren't for children," her mom says. "Why don't you stay home that night?"

Hazel's mom has a cloud of pale hair that she burns dry every morning. Whenever Hazel meets her focus, her frown springs into a grin. The grin is toothy and tight, like a sad shark that smiles only because of its anatomy.

"I never get to see the year change," Hazel says. "You never stay up."

"It's nothing special," her dad says. "You count down, you cheer. You might sing a song, if you're lucky. Best to just stay home."

Hazel clomps up to her room, chewing on a frightening urge to yell at him. She lets Ratty out, pets his back until her breathing slows. He's a shrunken cow, with his chocolate splashes on white fur. His muzzle is substantial for a rodent, his cascade of whiskers intelligent. He has a window of white in each dark eye.

He skitters across her bed, measuring. When he knows he's trapped, he settles on the quilt, hiding his face with his tail.

The next day is December thirtieth. Hazel, Melissa, and Kit meet on the ramp of I-95 to flash the oncoming lanes, forming a row ten feet from the shoulder. Melissa calls, "Three, two, one, flash!" and they lift their shirts. The idea is based on a Boston radio program that says on Wednesdays you have to flash cars if the bumper sticker says WOW. WOW means Whip 'em Out Wednesday. But they don't wait for the stickers.

They've been flashing since the summer, when it felt

beachy and warm. Hazel loved the feeling of the sun heating a part of her that hadn't touched fresh air since she was tiny. But they haven't been able to go the last few Wednesdays because it's already almost dark when school ends. Now that it's Christmas vacation, they can get here early enough.

Hazel has to unstrap her snow pants so the bib flaps down and unbutton her flannel and then untuck her T-shirt in preparation. Wind slides through the gaps in the cloth and stings her skin. All this work is too much, since there's no point in the endeavor anyway, but Melissa and Kit don't hesitate. None of them wears a bra, though Kit's the only one who should. Kit shakes her torso so her breasts wave, nipples puckering in the cold.

"Something crazy happened at Esther Meng's last night," Melissa says, rolling her eyes.

"Really?" Hazel hadn't known Melissa and Kit were going there.

"I was sitting on this guy's knees and he started jerking off. Kit was laughing and I was like, 'What?'"

Hazel pictures Melissa perched on the skinny legs of some boy. She wishes she'd been there to see how a guy could reach into his pants and snap the day open with sharp thrill. She was probably in bed at the time, staring at Ratty. "Who was the guy?"

"I don't know," Melissa says. "Some guy Rob. From the other high school."

"He's got this beautiful mushroom cut," says Kit. "The color of literal gold."

"Minuteman Tech?" Hazel asks. "Or the private school?"

"Minuteman Tech."

Hazel has more questions, but Kit screams, "Three, two, one, flash!"

Hazel strains to watch Melissa's body out of the corner of her eye. Although she and Hazel are equally flat, Melissa's shoulders sit back, her chest stuck out, and her skin is exactly one soft color.

As stupid as this is, Hazel's never considered how someone they know could see them flashing. Though she can't read license plates from this angle, the highway feels full of people journeying from Rhode Island to New Hampshire, skipping Massachusetts altogether. She never thought before that there might be a driver from Lexington or even their neighborhood, the Ridge. The idea ices through her, and she steps back from Melissa and Kit. When Melissa says, "Flash!" Hazel only lifts her shirt above her belly. Horns ring, and tires spit slush. Exhaust clogs her nostrils. The sky dims.

"Do you guys want to come over and train the rat?" Hazel asks. Melissa loves Ratty, jokes that one day she'll have his rodent-headed baby. The three of them crowd on Hazel's bed with the rat in the middle, calling, "Ratty, Ratty, Ratty." Whoever Ratty goes to is named Superior Trainer and chooses the next skill. Sometimes they each give Ratty a lychee and watch him peel it with his incisors, excavating the soggy eyeball. Whoever's lychee he opens first is Superior Trainer. Sometimes they put Ratty down Kit's pants.

Usually they place him in the sweaty crotch of her jeans, but sometimes, when Melissa is Superior Trainer, she puts Ratty straight in the underwear. Kit likes it. If she can stand the sensation for one minute, she's Superior Trainer, and if she can't then Melissa is. When Melissa's over, Hazel's house turns bright and furious.

"Not today," Melissa says. "Tomorrow's the party. I want to be rested. Woburn Anthony's going to be there."

"Who's Woburn Anthony?" Hazel asks. He sounds like a child star.

Melissa swipes at her hair, though it's not in her face. "He's a ninth-grade guy that's hot. From Woburn."

"You'll like him," Kit says. "He talks like a teenager already. Like, all slow. And he likes peas."

Hazel remembers her father shaking his wrinkled head, as though even asking about the party was infinitely disappointing. "I can't go."

Melissa sticks her hip out. Her sweatshirt is stretched at the bottom from all the yanking up and down. "Why not?"

"You didn't ask your parents, did you?" says Kit.

"You asked your *parents*?" says Melissa.

"They might've said yes. It's better than not asking."

"No, it's not," Melissa says. "Because now when you go they're going to be all leering into the hallway. Otherwise, they wouldn't have suspected crap."

"Well, it doesn't matter, because I can't go." The words sicken her. She hadn't accepted that Melissa and Kit would have the night without her. She kicks a sandwich, abandoned on the shoulder. The bread snaps off, revealing slick, icy ham and the wet lace of lettuce.

"Fine," says Melissa. "I know you want us to convince you, but whatever. Don't come. See if we care." She turns with a flourish and cuts through the grass back to the Ridge. There's no snow solid enough to stomp out now. Kit shrugs, sucks her teeth, and follows.

Hazel expects Melissa to come back and fight. They didn't even get to the yelling part yet. If Melissa tried, she could find an argument Hazel couldn't refuse. Hazel sits on the ground and watches the traffic.

The evening goes fuzzy. Puddles on the highway firm up, so the spray is gone. This is the time of day her father says it's hardest to see colors. She squints to identify the drivers, but none of them are familiar. They don't look like they live anywhere around here.

The next night is New Year's Eve. Hazel sits on her bed in a T-shirt with giggling sunflowers, her bangs smeared with the day's sweat. She thought if she put on pajamas, she'd get used to the idea of staying home, but instead she's just embarrassed of her sour, worn-out sleep shirt, as though Melissa and Kit can see her from across town.

Ratty turns in her cupped palms like a rag in the laundry, cleaning peanut butter from her thumb. She tries not to picture Melissa and Kit squirting glitter on their cheeks and perfume on their crotches. At nine her dad floats into the doorway.

"Happy New Year," he says with exaggerated kindness.

She gives a thumbs-up, because she doesn't have the heart to make her face look cheerful. He grabs the lintel and shakes his head, looking older than ever. White hairs sprout from his eyebrows. They're silky, tickling the air.

Hazel's mom trades places with him. She's had her bath, and her hair is slicked back like an otter's, spines sticking up where her comb passed through. She points to the cage, and Hazel tucks her rat away.

"Listen, Haze," she says, like she might sit down, but she doesn't. "Next year you can go to a party. And it'll be special that way because it'll be the year 2000." She looks pleased, folding her hands over her stomach. Hazel wants to agree, wants to say she'll wait, that she'll spend a year thinking about how glorious life will be in 2000, when maybe she'll finally understand what's happening with the president. But there might not be a party next year, and, if there is, Hazel might not be invited. "But I want to go tonight."

Her mom shakes her head and says, "You're tired."

"I'm not."

Her mom kisses her and leaves. There's murmuring in the hallway, then silence as her parents retreat into the master bedroom.

Hazel roots herself to the bed, willing herself to get tired, but she can't forget Melissa and Kit on the other side of town.

Every second they're bonding closer, building a wild, exciting community that she'll never even see. She'll at least put on her regular clothes. Then she'll feel less pathetic.

She puts on her jeans and flannel shirt. She straps into her snow pants. She rotates before the tarnished mirror with the painted fruit bowl that her dad let her choose at a long-ago flea market. She shoves her bangs out of her eyes. She looks like she's going out. She's going out.

If her mom knew she was going to the party, her springy smile would fall. And if anything bothers Hazel more than the smile, it's the smile breaking.

But Melissa's face yesterday was scrunched into a fist. She's on the verge of hating Hazel. If Melissa hates her, Kit will too, even if she doesn't want to. Hazel will have to eat school lunch again in the utility room the way she did before Melissa discovered her in Home Ec at the beginning of the year, reaching over and manipulating the dough of Hazel's tea cake until it sat correctly in the pan. But why wouldn't Melissa want a new life? That boy stroking himself while Melissa balanced on his knees. How crazy that is. How exciting, in a way.

She lifts Ratty by the tail and swings him, his claws pulsing to grip air. His bored eyes and active nose soothe her. If she took him with her, at least she'd have some comfort. She feeds him a crumb of Tylenol PM and drops him in her pocket, securing the snap.

She slides into the hallway, her back to the wall. Her parents' door is ajar. She swings her right foot out in a long arc before setting it carefully on the dusty wood and sliding her left foot to meet it. She arrives at the top of the steps, her knees jiggling in their sockets. The staircase is a craggy tunnel, needlessly steep, as though the pilgrims required hardship even in their own homes.

She lowers her foot to the first step, holds her breath, and shifts her weight. The house is still. She makes her way down the stairs, avoiding the hollow spots that even Ratty can activate. One sound and her father would be on her, leaking disappointment, shaming her back to bed.

Grabbing her boots from the foyer, an eyelet strikes the hinge of the French door. The sound is tiny but clear, like a dropped earring. She waits for the shells of echo to peel away. She bites her lip, ready for her father's voice, hoarsely calling—hoping for it, even—but there's only silence.

A full minute passes before she absorbs that there's only the beat of the highway in the distance. She can't even hear her parents breathe. She carries her boots outside and ties them on the stoop, her hands trembling so hard that she knots her finger in twice. She checks the window of the master bedroom. Just snow falling against dark glass.

Every step she takes away from the front door, she expects her father to catch her by her snow pants strap. He's been strict all her life, and she's been careful to follow his rules. Now she's broken one so easily. Loneliness sweeps her. No one's watching. When she snaps through the crust of snow and walks away from the house, a chill tickles her. She shouldn't be allowed to just leave.

•

The neighborhood is muffled and white. Everyone has their lights on, and TVs cheer through fastened windows. Couples hunch into cars, powdered sugar dusted on black suits and dresses. Esther's house is by the town center, Melissa said, off the fork. Hazel heads north.

She walks a mile, seeking kids dressed for a party. Near the center she spots two boys. They don't look old enough for high school, but Minuteman Tech starts in eighth grade.

The boys turn off at the apartment building by the gas station, and Hazel remembers: Piney Haven. That's the address Kit repeated a hundred times in the last two weeks that sounds like a fine-smelling coffin. The complex presses up against a grove of blue firs planted so densely you'd have to squeeze to fit between them. She watches from a distance as the boys pull open the door to a unit.

Hazel wishes she'd come with Melissa and Kit. She'd have stayed close until she grew brave enough to wander alone among the crowds. And she shouldn't have brought Ratty. He scrambles against her leg, trying to pass the pocket snap, his movements dulled by medicine.

No music or cheering broadcasts from the apartment. No one is singing. Kit and one of the Minuteman boys come out and sit in the snow on the concrete step to share a cigarette. Kit has smoked biweekly since she was eleven. Sometimes she smokes half, then packs the butt in a candy tin for later. She's shaved her head again, this time down to the skin.

47

When Hazel is halfway to the steps, Kit shouts, "Hazel!" the word shooting to Hazel's heart. She'd been scared Kit would ignore her around her new friends, but Kit throws an arm over Hazel's shoulder, driving her into the ground.

"You came," Kit says. "That's so dope. This is Rob."

Kit's arm is heavy and comforting on Hazel's shoulders, cozy in the snowy night. The face of the boy in question peeks from behind a knotted fringe of bangs. This is the boy whose knees Melissa sat on. He's exactly like Hazel pictured: soft face, thick nose, elbows poking from holes in his sleeves. He releases a mouth-shaped packet of smoke. "Nice pants."

"Wow," Kit says. "Aren't we having fun?" She steers Hazel toward the front door. "It's party time."

Hazel gathers force into her voice. "This is magnificent."

The apartment opens into a living room with a gray couch pushed against the wall, and a threshold beyond that leads to a kitchen with a particleboard table. On the table rests a pizza box with one slice left, cheese glue sealing it to the cardboard. A girl sits on the couch, her hair bleached orange, with black roots. She holds a wineglass topped off with a brown, bubbly drink. She's too rodenty to be Esther Meng, almost a nerd. But the couch curls around her back like it's conformed to her body over years.

"Welcome to the best party of the nineteen hundreds," she says, pressing the rim of the glass to Hazel's chin.

"No thanks." Hazel speaks as clearly as possible with the glass denting her mouth. "Where's Melissa?"

Esther doesn't remove the glass.

"Esther," Kit says. "Cut it out."

But this is Esther's party, and Hazel can't ignore her. She takes a sip, and her mouth burns with flavorless poison. Her feet loosen in her boots, and she sways. She grabs Esther's shoulder to steady herself.

"You're precious," Esther says, pressing a blue nail into Hazel's cheek and sliding it along the curve of her jaw. "I think I'll eat you out."

Esther watches Hazel in an intent way. Not like Melissa or Kit, because there's always the other to split the energy. With Esther it's like Hazel's the only one in the room. Hazel holds her gaze, proud and steady, testing the feeling of being worthy. Esther tucks a chunk of hair behind her ear. She's ragged under the eyes in an appealing way, like she knows all about adulthood and beyond: old age, disappointment, death. Like she's sat around the table with every fear. Hazel needs her secrets. Right now. She steps closer, but Kit pulls her back.

"Hazel has her period," Kit says. She looks as worried as she did the day Hazel stumbled off the shoulder into I-95, flashing a battered utility van.

"I don't," Hazel says.

Kit jerks Hazel away. "Come on, idiot."

They settle together in the kitchen. Esther stays in the living room, but she's visible through the threshold, picking nail polish from her thumb. Kit pinches cheese off the last slice of pizza, arranging the specks into a dotted line. Any minute a horde will burst through the door, laughing and singing New Year's songs, Melissa at the center.

"We thought you weren't coming," Kit says. "Melissa was like, 'Fuck her. She thinks she's better than us.'"

"No, I don't." Hazel opens her pocket and fondles Ratty. He must look pink in there, with the light diffusing through the nylon. "I stink."

Kit rests her head on the table. "Melissa might do it tonight. You know. Like *do* it. For real."

"She means full sex," Esther drones from across the threshold.

Hazel pictures Melissa tangled with Rob, breathing like she ran the mile at school. She shakes her head, but the image presses in, fleshy and sour.

As though conjured, Rob enters the kitchen and thrusts his hips at Kit. Automatically she handles his crotch, mashing it like a stress ball. Hazel covers her mouth to avoid yelling out, but Rob looks natural, gazing at a chip in the wall. The coat of paint underneath was tangerine, a spark against the current beige.

"Wait," Hazel says. "I thought you were a lesbian."

"I am," says Kit.

When Kit moved to Lexington at age eleven, she was already out to her parents and her whole Montessori school. Kit invited Hazel and Melissa to a sleepover at the beginning of this year, before she really knew them. They sat on her bed eating Smartfood, and Kit said, "I have a personal secret."

But now, here in Esther's kitchen, Kit is manhandling

a penis and scrotum like it's nothing. Hazel says, "But that doesn't make any sense."

"Shut it," says Rob.

Hazel goes unsteady, gripping her chair with both hands. Kit's wide face is flushed, eyebrows raised, nose crinkled. What have Kit and Melissa been doing in this house all these weeks? Are they lost to Hazel already? Kit's expression is unfamiliar, her mouth loose and accommodating. Hazel watches her fingers, memorizing the pattern of her kneading, in case later she has to perform the task herself.

A door off the living room flies open, cracking against the plaster to reveal a woman in a nightgown. As soon as Hazel can bend her knees, stiff with the shock of seeing a grown-up here, she ducks under the table. This woman will certainly call her father. He'll yell at her for the whole drive home. She's comforted by the idea of the dark car: dry heat cycling through the vents, her father's possessive anger, his heavy palming of the wheel.

From where Hazel crouches under the table, the woman looms tall, the base of her chin bobbing as she speaks to Esther in another language, indicating the door that Rob left open. The nightgown blows around her like tissue, and she clutches it at her throat. Hazel retreats further until all she can see are the woman's toes, painted the color of her skin.

The woman takes a step toward Esther, placing her feet carefully and solidly, as though on the deck of a ship. Esther yells a sharp word. The woman spins and slams herself back inside.

"Don't listen to her," Esther says as Hazel climbs back into her chair. "She thinks she's still in Cambodia."

Hazel wonders what Esther's word was, if she could use it on her own parents, if she could even pronounce it. She imagines shouting the word at her father, his head springing back on his spine, eyes brightening in their nests of beige skin. She can't steady herself on the chair knowing there's a mother here who's unable to change the course of the party. The front door is still open, snowflakes absorbing into the armchair.

"Can we close the door?" Hazel asks, but Esther and Kit ignore her. The heat from the baseboards bleeds into the night, and Hazel jams her arms under the waistband of her snow pants and her normal pants so they clench her naked thighs.

The pantry door opens. Hazel is afraid it's more Mengs, that Esther's family will pop now from every crevice. But it's a boy with a black bob and a dent under one eye, like someone pushed their thumb in, hard. His shoulders curl forward, and he walks like a weasel, tense and sly.

"Hey, Anthony," Kit says. "Having fun?"

Anthony snorts, and Melissa steps from the pantry, yellow hair flashing. It's uncool to smile, but Hazel can't help it. Melissa's already here. They all are. So what if they're at Esther Meng's? They've never cared if they're on the highway or in the graveyard or in Hazel's room with her parents reading downstairs: wherever they are, the three of them build their own world. They can reach that place here as well as anywhere.

"Hey, Melissa," Hazel says.

Melissa rolls her eyes and laughs at Anthony, though he didn't make a joke. Her mouth is shiny around her lips, and her eyes are agate marbles, hard but pretty. They flicker, and Hazel's breath catches. But Melissa walks the other way and curls up on the couch decorated with snowflakes from the open door. Wind wrinkles her hair. She's a lioness, golden and proud and easy with danger.

Hazel scrambles for any scrap that will remind Melissa they're friends. Some secret that only the three of them know. "Hey, Melissa. I have an idea."

"Congratulations." Melissa watches the wall as if it were a TV, focused on a bloom of mold. Her hair is washed of its yellow by the fluorescent overhead. Hazel twists in her seat. She longs for Melissa's mouth to twitch like it does right before she orders Hazel to pin Kit to the ground, one wet tooth flashing. But Melissa's face is set, her concentration drilling into the mold. She's willfully forgetting Hazel, and even Kit. After all Kit lets them do to her, Melissa should at least acknowledge her.

Hazel sits forward. She can't merely say hi. She has to remind Melissa who she is. "Let's do a practice sex," she says, her voice as strident as a parent's.

Kit releases a low hoot, and Esther covers her mouth too late to block a snort.

"Oh shit," Esther says. "Melissa's been *revealed*."

Melissa turns to Hazel, hair flinging over her shoulder. Her nose and cheeks burn rashy red. "What are you talking about?"

Hazel shudders, but her voice comes out clear. "You know. Like at Sacred Heart." The whole room is listening now, even the walls bending toward her. The boys are open-mouthed, feebly laughing. Esther leans forward like she wants to join the fight.

"When we put Kit on the ground and you tell me to hold her wrists." She'll explain it all if they let her: the corners of Kit's bones cutting into Hazel's palms, the static in the air, the clouds pressing on her back, snow ready to drop. Melissa's finger pushing into Kit, shallow, then deep, then too deep, that swish of moisture and that sound Kit makes, halfway between murmur and growl, like a song to which Hazel wishes she knew the words, the graves rising around Melissa like men, gray and featureless. Melissa's face over Kit's naked groin, gazing at Hazel. Kit's head resting on its thin cushion of hair, her expression faraway. All Hazel has to do is hold Kit's wrists and she's part of all that.

"You're insane," Melissa says, her voice tumbling out wildly. "I never realized this before, but you're literally insane, aren't you?"

Hazel pushes back against her chair and stands. Anthony and Rob and Esther and Kit watch her like she's a dog that's slipped its collar and they don't know yet whether she'll run or attack or soil herself.

"Show us," Esther whispers, and it's like she can see into Hazel's mind.

"Come on," Hazel says. A push enters her voice. She takes Melissa's wrist, which is as cool and hard as plastic.

She expects Melissa to yank free, but she stiffens, her focus shifting between Anthony and Rob. As though they'd ever help. They just sit there, useless.

"Hazel," Kit says. "Watch it." But she won't get involved until she has to.

Now that Hazel has hold of Melissa, she should shove her to the floor, like the president pushing a cigar into the girl people say was a kid—though she looks more like a mom—standing back to admire what he'd made. She's about to say they should shut down the party, that the practice sex is too terrifying in the end, when Ratty swims against her hip. She doesn't stop him as he eases his body into the leg of her snow pants, fingernails poking through the nylon, spine brushing her shin, lowering himself all the way down her leg. Of course he's saving her. Of course.

He reaches her ankle and emerges from the cuff, paws starfished and clinging to the cotton of her socks. His head, emerging, is so painfully tiny and perfect that Hazel's eyes sting: those whiskers sparkling in the fluorescence, pink claws testing carpet, that nose so tender the flesh would break at one touch.

What will the days be now that Melissa and Kit are so far away? She'll return to the utility room for lunch, her chicken dripping on the bleached floor. She'll shut herself in there after school too, wait out the rush so she won't have to see Melissa and Kit off on some new journey. She wants to cry, but she can't. It's New Year's.

Outside the window, potassium lamps bake the snow in

lukewarm light. As Ratty's tail unravels out of Hazel's cuff, as Esther and Anthony suck in breath, Hazel clings tighter to Melissa's wrist, pulling it toward her chest. She concentrates on a distant sound, far beyond Esther's apartment: someone singing, miles away. The voices of people she doesn't know yet, their heads tipped to the sky, yelling for the next year, and all to come after that.

Pink Knives

WE MEET IN THE PLAGUE. YOUR GRAY ROOTS HAVE grown out four or five inches into the red—we're that deep in. We sit on opposite hips of a circle printed on the grass in a crowded public park in San Francisco. Around us are first-date kisses, teens huddled dangerously close together on tarps, techies dancing to rubberized jewel-toned radios. Everyone massing into Dolores Park for whatever they need: sex, friendship, family, work meetings, chess lessons, air, rigorous jump rope, letting their toddlers scream like wolves, pudgy arms extended, anticipating a fall. Toddlers who will grow up warped by this time, unused to the touch of peers.

The park is the only place to go. No one too concerned about the real reason their lives have shifted—a reason that dangles in the famous fog and sticks to fomites everywhere— everyone, like me, scraping out what pleasures they can. Even with a friend in the ICU, I forget. Even with her daily pictures: hospital pancakes, views of the bay, the mysterious clear plastic device named Voldyne, like a fancy lady, that opens her lungs. She's getting worse. You let your two-toned bangs fall over your eyes and look askance: smoky, haunted. I like that. I want to know why.

This is our first meeting. You've been furloughed that day from your job as a government asylum officer. You use my right pronouns. You ask my sign and whether I have "sexual vitality." I say yes, though I'm not sure, exactly, what it means. Whatever it is, I have it. I haven't seen my girlfriend for six months—she's stuck across the country, afraid to travel because of a skin tag blocking her trachea. We've opened our relationship. Her choice, my treat. This is the first try. Your father has died. I never learn when or how. I want to ask. There's a picture of him on your refrigerator. Coney Island, late eighties. You, dark-haired, pigtails, eyes bright then, straddling your bicycle with your feet flat on the sidewalk, handlebars tricked out with a purple horn. He, hiding behind sunglasses and a baggy charcoal suit, like he knew he'd be gone one day and wanted to hide himself from scrutiny, his hand resting on the back wheel of your bike so lightly that you wouldn't have known you weren't keeping yourself upright if it weren't for this picture taken in an instant in that part of the middle of an afternoon where the light is ugly and stark, even in the city. This picture you face every time you retrieve frozen cookies, fancy cheese, beer.

Your apartment has paintings of cupcakes and rainbows and tigers on the walls, all this neon cheer to hide the fact that the windows open onto bricks and masturbation sounds pipe in from unknown sources and a teenager lives next door

who screams at you to go fuck yourself. You won't fuck yourself today. Or at least, not only.

I've been touched once since the plague began. My friend
Eve, visiting from Portland on her way to buy a house in
Joshua Tree—Twentynine Palms, really—a little home-
steader's cabin under the lights of the military base. She
stood by the fence in front of my apartment on the Berkeley–
Oakland border and said, "Are you ready?" I said, "Yes," because I was, for anything, I'd been alone so long I was going
crazy. I had no idea what Eve was readying me for, until she
sprang across the distance between us and hugged me, wrapping me in overheated funk from sitting in a white Prius too
long in June with only one stop for gas all the way from Oregon. Endorphins raced through me like heroin and I swear I
felt good from her touch for weeks.

More than a hug is on the table now. We've deserted the
park for your apartment on Valencia. You are standing by
the couch, head forward because you lead with your nose,
posture deteriorating this early in the quarantine because
you refuse to have a desk in your apartment, stubbornly ap-
proving citizenship on your couch, leaning way too far over
files full of people's best versions of themselves, though a
desk is the only furniture I'd have if I had to choose. I'd sleep
under it like a dog. I'd eat on it, I'd bow to it like a television.
I'm a masochist and a workaholic, but you can't tell yet. You
don't hate me for it yet.

The mask on your face dances with tiny pink butcher
knives. I'm obsessed with those soft pastel blades and I look

the mask up later online and buy it and never tell you, even when my girlfriend buys it too, after seeing it on my face. If another plague comes, which it will, if this one lasts and lasts, which it will, my girlfriend and I, united sometime far from now in New Jersey or the East Bay, will hold hands with matching knives slicing across our muzzles, and will we think of you? Will my heart rip a little, thinking of you? Will my girlfriend even know enough details to begin? What will I dare tell her? Is this the kind of weird shit you mean when you say you don't want to date someone in a relationship?

The year before the plague, I lived in Krakow, the most polluted city in Europe. Whenever my air purifier glowed red or purple, I wore a mask down Starowiślna and across the park that used to be the city walls, my dziękujęs muffled behind reinforced cloth. Passing the shops whose pluralization made any item cute: lampy, tablety, chipsy, komputery. I longed for America, where I'd never wear a mask again. My last act in Poland was trashing a gallon bag of N95s in the Warsaw airport. Now I smell my breath all day against my face, on endless walks, afraid to touch my phone and contaminate it, but caving for updates from the ICU, where the onset of twilight makes the virus worse, because the immune system accelerates at night, my friend says, or her doctor, her chest compacted with sediment, her oxygen dialed high: *It's almost five. The hour my lungs fail.* Sometimes I forget to worry about her and my whole body goes rigid as if I've cursed her and I light another candle, a Catholic habit borrowed from my girlfriend. I hold the tapered green wax as the flame swallows oxygen.

You say, "I wish I could invite you to stay and relax." This is a normal thing to say. But what you do not know is that I never relax. I walk sixteen miles a day. I write a hundred more stories than I can sell. I water a flowerbox of lettuces that I never feel like I deserve to harvest. It's never time to finish and enjoy, even a tiny bitter red leaf. I have hemorrhoids and acid reflux and pits in my feet eaten by bacteria. But it's kind of nice, kind of quaint, that you ask, even if it shows how little you know me, and I like it. I've used your bathroom. That's why we're here. You haven't condemned me to the facilities on Church with girls giggling so close behind me in line that the virus dampens the back of my neck, and I'm grateful. But now I'm in your living room that's also your bedroom and you're telling me I can't stay. And the mask on my face presses my breath against my teeth and the mask with the knives covers your face in a way that's fetching, not that I don't like your face, but it intensifies your smoky eyes when they're all I have to read.

I can't reach out to touch you. You're furloughed, but just, and you've talked face-to-face with several dozen pending citizens today and every day for weeks. You don't like it. You're afraid you'll get sick. But it's important. This is cynical, you say, but not the least because of all those votes. November is coming. The plague has put us hundreds of thousands of new citizens behind. No one's touched you for eighteen weeks, three weeks longer than I've gone, because of

Eve's hug. You said, on the circle in the park, that you're "not a physical person," which worried me, but here we are, leaning toward each other, talking about how we can't touch, and blood knifes through me. I can't even breathe. The first time I might touch anyone new in a decade. An exposed person—this shouldn't turn me on. People are dying. People I know. My friend clutching Voldyne and wishing five would never come. It shouldn't turn me on that there's no future for us because of my girlfriend. It's doomed, this thing with you, like the rest of the world. I shouldn't be here, in a stranger's apartment, but you already don't look like a stranger, the way you turn your head and laugh silently when I say something off-color. You're like my older friends: cool, sour girls on the tail end of Gen X, with their hoodies like yours and their plague-canceled Bikini Kill tickets like yours, but this is different, this is new, and you told me on the app you weren't sure about me, that you've dated other people—girls, but we won't say girls—in relationships already and it hasn't worked. I've considered the pitfalls, of course I have, but different ones—disease—who's not thinking about disease right now—my girlfriend's jealousy, mine, which is worse—I'm a Scorpio, I've told you so already and still you're standing here—but not, ever, have I worried about someone liking me too much, which suddenly seems possible in this dark, peaceful apartment, no sign of the Mission up here, not even the distant ocean hum of Valencia.

And then you take off your mask. It's dirty. It's a dirty thing to do. In two different but related ways. Your mouth and nose are body parts I shouldn't see inside a room: exposed, fleshy, freshened with sweat. My blood knifes again. Your smile—I know from photographs, but I forgot—is gummy but wise, mocking. You say, "This is going to be illegal," and I know, the way I didn't know when Eve asked, "Are you ready?" that I'm about to be touched, and this time the endorphins come early, because I understand now, for the first time since my long, lonely childhood, what it means to be touched after months, and my pleasure rises to meet you.

You reach my shoulder first. I don't remove my mask, though your face is close, asking. I pull down the fabric. We kiss. Almost, it's too much. Not like Eve's hug, not like nerves everywhere cooperating to light up, but scary, as if this threat I've guarded against for months, sanitizing my hands and spraying bleach on my phone and kicking the gate open, letting the mail percolate for a day, three if it has tape, texting my friend in the ICU if I haven't heard from her in three hours, forsaking everything I used to love—classrooms and parties and restaurants and adventure and my girlfriend most of all—and now I'm smashing my mouth against the mouth of a stranger and my spine kicks back against the shock.

You don't notice. And I relax. Your touch does it, on my shoulders, my back, and now—are we moving this fast?—my chest.

"Is this okay?" you ask.

"They'll be gone soon anyway," I say.

"What's gone?" Your voice is groggy, like you're asleep.

"My chest," I say, because I can't pronounce any of the smorgasbord of the other goofier and more vivid terms available. "I'm getting surgery. On December third." And then I add, "2020," like the year was ever in question. Like anyone could forget this year. Like I'm not aware of all the new ways along with the old that the procedure will put me at risk.

"Can I touch them now?" you ask. "While they're here on earth?" which is bold, but maybe you feel the way I feel, that certain things are possible now, with you, that cannot happen anywhere else. Like this is the whole point.

I should say no. My therapist would advise me, in her firm, intimidating way, to say no. I tell my girlfriend no, which makes her sad. She loves that part of my body, and her love haunts me at every stage of surgery: taking tawdry pictures of myself for the remote consult—my bathtub in the background, containing one dusty puddle—the remote consult itself with the hold message about liposuction and eye work, the before-and-after pictures of strangers baldly lit and uncomfortable, shoulders hunched around bruises, the follow-up to the remote consult. Collecting a letter from my therapist, pushing on my insurance, pushing on the surgeon, scheduling a date, buying compression vests and scar strips and shea butter and silicone and pineapple, all this effort just to steal some of my girlfriend's joy. Especially now, it seems cruel, when she's all alone, when we're without each other. When I have very little to offer as it is. But, December third. It's not certain, but I'm proud of it. Knowing all this, I still say, "Yes."

You peel off my T-shirt. You toss it on the couch where you approve citizenship. On your sunset cushion, under the painting of a neon tiger, it's a withered casing, like how could it contain me? Then the binder. You use your nails to pry it from my skin, where sweat has sealed it. My binder that has broken a rib or two but that makes me ecstatic anyway, in an embarrassingly childish way, whenever I pull it on, so much so that I'd never take it off if it didn't stop me from breathing and digesting food. You do not hesitate in any of this. I want to be clear. You remove both layers with a hard set to your mouth. And since you've used my right pronoun, which my girlfriend can't always quite get, which I can't always quite get, which confuses and upsets my friends, to what extent they think about me or it at all, which my family won't know about until they read this story, whatever final form it takes, I assume what you are doing is right. That you, older than me, living this queer, fatherless life in the Mission, full of friends that light you up when you talk about them, because they are your real family, so much more so than your mother who's a hermit and your brothers who treat you like a child, that whole constellation back in Concy Island where you never, ever visit, that you might know better than I know what I need right now. Or maybe I need someone to follow.

You've been tender when you touched me before. Too much so. A feathery touch, too affectionate, makes me squirm. But when you touch my chest now, it's firm, exacting, like you want to know the shape, and what's inside, to measure what I'll lose. Sometimes I imagine the scar, jagged and wine red, crusty with old blood, terrifying my girlfriend as she bathes me even as she pretends it doesn't, steadying her hands on the sponge on my spine, and I think about the mornings I got up early from age eleven on to slice my fingers under the nail bed with a razor, my wrists, my upper arms. I stored the razor in my Pillsbury Doughboy doll, graduated to scratching through the skin until I'd left ointment-yellow patches beading with blood. My parents said nothing because they thought the habit was "private." My therapist said to consider the scar a sign I finally did what I wanted with my body, but I don't know if I can.

You're absorbed in touching me. You're not looking at me anymore, only at the part of me that will soon be gone. I've deserted this transaction. The part in your hair is pink where the gray roots meet scalp, in a way that never would've been visible with the red dye you've applied since age fifteen. Before we met you told me about your roots. You said you didn't feel sexy now, because of your roots. You sent a picture, yourself in the knife mask, lying on your spine in Dolores Park, stroking the chin of a dog who I'd hoped was yours but isn't. I told you I liked your hair like that, and I do. It looks crazy, but I do. There are freckles high in your part. Two, huddled in their gray forest. Do you know they're there? I touch them, lightly, with one finger.

You take it as an order. You hunch down and suck a nipple. You haven't noticed yet that I have five nipples, in two rows, like a dog. My girlfriend is the only one who ever noticed. I didn't for my first twenty-eight years of life, because I avoided that part of me. I didn't believe her, but the surgeon said she was right; that it was normal enough. He laughed. "If we lose one, you'll still have four."

I hate you sucking me, though you can't know this. All my sensation, electric and painful, gathers in my nipple that will soon be removed, a coin of skin, and laid on a hygienic table, awaiting grafting. But now it is attached, attaching us, and I'm so skinless I could fall apart. This is the first time I hate myself in this whole experiment. This is the first time I cross the line. And it's not about the lines that should matter. Not all the ways we might spread the virus. Not my friend in the ICU, about to be intubated. Not all the ways we'll destroy each other in the next hour, or, if not, soon, inevitably. But because I haven't let my girlfriend do this for years, and she wants to, and she's alone in New Jersey with her blocked throat, waiting for the world to get less dangerous. I should stop you. That's the least decency I could offer. When you read this, you'll feel so bad. Especially since some of this is not exactly true, while most of it is exactly true. Maybe for you, none of it is. But, for now, the strip of scalp between your roots is under me, pink and vulnerable, your back arched like it is every day over documents in your sunless apartment, alone, and I don't say a thing.

A Fearless Moral Inventory

CARLA PROMISES HERSELF AND POOJA FROM THE LI-
brary that she won't engage with the Mifflin Street Fair tomorrow, won't drink with the undergrads, won't even walk
down her street while it's in session, though her apartment
and the library are both on Mifflin—a chilly length of resi-
dential Wisconsin street that's raucous once a year. Carla has
a sex addiction, but she's been perfect for a month, and she
resolves to maintain.

Pooja offers a half-assed solution: a vacation to the Dells
for the day. She presents the idea like it's just occurred to
her. "You could get a room on the waterpark side," she says,
falsely casual, her busybody hands herding the due-date
stamps into a row. "Rates are a joke in the off-season. And
this one hotel has a slide straight from the main office into
the pool."

Carla pictures herself in her stretched-out bikini, selected to showcase the most flesh and not the least bit flattering, pitching out of a hotel on a water slide, in full view of
Route 13. She promises Pooja that she won't repeat 2014. No
way, not this year. She has the ferrets.

"I'm a mom now," she says.

Pooja freshens the knot on her scarf and offers a worried smile. "I'll cover for you at the library. I rearranged my schedule."

"That's ridiculous. I'll be fine."

Carla hunches from Pooja's sagging grin and squanders her fifteen-minute break gazing at the expanse of Mifflin, pristine from the street sweeper. A wobbly copy of herself watches back from the plate glass window across the road.

The next morning, the sun is a red rip on the horizon, gilding the doughnut of the sleeping ferrets in their cage. The fair has already started. Outside, a girl spins a hula hoop around her skinny hips. Glitter courses through the tube like a mini river. She must be cold out there, in her tank top. Though it's technically spring, the snow only melted a few days before.

Carla has been attending Sex and Love Addiction Anonymous meetings for three years. In Madison, her home meeting is held in the basement of the community center. She goes every week. Or at least every other. Though she was humiliated to tell Pooja, Annie, and Linda—all new friends, all librarians—that she'd become involved with the program—part of her self-assigned Accountability Homework—she has to admit that the meetings make sense. SLA is definitely what she has. She likes sex, obviously, comes easily and is rarely grossed out. What gets her is the urgent penny romance of one-night stands. A guy she doesn't even know becoming moved enough to sweep her bangs away, a baby dyke's hungry grip. People are startled by how much they like her. She's chubby, with big lips and a childish laugh.

Some symptoms on the SLAA website seem universal. Like lacking boundaries and fearing loneliness. Who has boundaries, truly? Who likes loneliness? Carla doesn't understand how the opposite kind of people—people who fear sex and avoid intimacy—fall into the same addiction category. Her eyes glaze when members launch into sagas of pizza and milk at home on a Saturday night. Is she supposed to be surprised because they're hot? One tenet says SLAs sexualize stress and guilt. She can almost put her finger on that one, but not quite.

Carla's sponsor, Shawna, brays that Carla can call anytime, though Carla never does. Shawna hugs her at the beginning and end of each meeting, whispers into her hair that she's proud, which stings Carla's eyes. Carla tells herself she doesn't need a sponsor, that her friendship with Pooja is enough. But Pooja nods briskly whenever Carla explains how difficult it is to resist going out alone to the Old Fashioned, the Weary Traveler, Plan B. Pooja wrinkles her eyelids when Carla shares her fantasies about their manager, Martha. "Really?" she asks. She burps a laugh when Carla gestures to an undergrad, sprawled on a puffy chair, that she can't stop staring at. Carla's never told Pooja about Dave.

In the three years since Dave, Carla has had thirty official relationships. She stopped counting one-night stands when she got to a hundred. Over a hundred seemed egregious, though she's certainly doubled that number by now.

Carla lets the ferrets out of their cage. They charge like spring-loaded slinkies, bounding over dirty laundry and setting pawprints in butter and infusing the air with musky cheer. She bought them on impulse two months ago from the strip mall in Monona, where she was getting waxed. Shawna had recommended she get a pet, and a sign fixed to the window said: THREE FERRETS. Nothing was more depressing than the powdered meat odor and ratty sawdust-stuffed dogs at the Dane County Pet Shop. Her mission was wax, then rescue. Three ferrets sounded extreme, but one was cruel. She sometimes mulls over the ferret she didn't buy. He was fat and tummy-bald, without the traditional mask. The light fur around his eyes made him too human. Carla didn't want that creep watching her while she lived her life. Still, she feels bad. She took all his friends. She wonders if anyone ever came for him.

Boo is so creamy he's yellow, fluffier, sweeter. Cody, a prairie sable, prefers bouncing around the apartment on private errands, while Boo always wants to play. The playing involves a series of nips delivered at high speed, though, so Carla prefers Cody.

She scoops Cody up. "Come on, Codeine. Let's watch TV." Carla clicks the remote and the TV pops to life on a gameshow where contestants have to name their darkest fear and greatest wish. The fears and wishes are heralded with equally saturated, blinding graphics.

If Carla were on the show, she'd wish for Dave. Not that he'd come back, because he would if she called. She'd wish she'd handled the situation better when he got raped, or sexually assaulted, or whatever it was. She wishes she'd believed him and sided with him wholeheartedly. She doesn't know her darkest fear. She might not have one. That's maybe the problem.

Carla holds back, but ultimately she can't stop herself from calling Pooja. "Can you really cover?" Pooja never agrees to cover for her, since Carla works in the Buzzman Reading Room, which is an alleged cruising area. Pooja prefers her exalted post at Reference, picking out computer keys with a high back, as though each patron were a full professor, when most are the same sleepy students in sweatpants and dirty headbands.

"I just don't want to, like, travel to the library," Carla says. This isn't technically a lie.

"That's sensible," Pooja says. "You're finally making responsible decisions for yourself."

Carla wants badly for Pooja to call bullshit, but Pooja uses her standard flat, half-distracted tone. Either she doesn't care or she actually believes Carla. Sometimes Carla scares herself with how easy it is to lie.

Carla tries to forget the last fair, but she can't help it. All year she's told herself stories of last winter, psyching herself up not to go this time. Now the scenes fill her with greedy anticipation. Mifflin Street Fair, of course, isn't the problem, just an environment where the problem thrives, like a slice of bread for a colony of mold. If she still wants to go, then it's immaterial whether she goes or not. The spores are there, so it doesn't matter if she sets them on spongy old bread. That's not the recovery line, but it makes a certain kind of sense.

Last winter was Carla's first in Madison. She was warned of a festival on her street for undergraduates, started in the sixties as a protest. She'd anticipated an innocent affair—fried dough, lemonade, chats about coursework. Instead, there she was, thirty-two years old, stumbling into a house with a banner specially welcoming freshmen, jerking down the pants of the closest guy. There was the bare wild-berry blue mattress in the next house, the short butch girl who told her she was a "rad lady." Those people are her neighbors. She has to look into the middle distance when they pass with hauls of malt liquor and corn chips. Some of them just finished high school. They're barely people.

But she's okay now. She's on step four, making a fearless moral inventory. She's taking solace and inspiration from friends. She's finding meaning in hobbies, if you count the ferrets. She's counting them toward another goal too: the goal of loving something more than you love yourself.

Carla longs to get out to the fair. Instead she heaves the ferret cage onto the kitchen counter and sets to cleaning it. She scrubs between the bars with an old foot brush, using pure bleach, the strongest cleaning component she owns. She hand-washes the hammock and refreshes the litter and water. She works for an hour. Once the cage sparkles, she sets it on towels in the corner of her living room. Then she waits for the ferrets to encounter their new home.

Boo hovers at the entrance before stepping inside. Carla waits for him to bound into the newly clean environment, to cuddle and roll in the fresh hammock, slipping in and out of its pocket, depositing a poop in the center of the snowy fields of litter. Instead he cranes his head into the food bowl. Which Carla forgot to wash. Which she forgot to stock with kibble.

A sigh blasts through her. She can't do anything right. She can't stand it—she has to get out. She's wearing leggings and a silky pajama top, which could pass for a club outfit in some circles, if she were slimmer. But she can't wait any longer or she'll go crazy. She slops kibble into the ferrets' bowls as fast as she can, stray pellets rattling to the floor, then lunges across the room to seize her coat.

Carla shakes the ferrets from her head as she hits the street. Sometimes she's tough and good but other times she's over-sensitive. She's disappointed by every holiday and by her friends losing touch when she moved. She's disappointed by Madison, a toy town with its railroad and lakes and State House on its tidy hill, its middle-class straight people smugly slapping rainbow stickers on every naked door. The kind of people she's afraid to tell she's pan, because then she has to prove all their prejudices right. She's disappointed by her job at the library, for not being more challenging without being harder. Even when she was most in love, she was still some-times disappointed by Dave, by the way she saw him through the eyes of other women, how they so easily laughed with him and swatted at him, even pressed in when they hugged him, right in front of Carla—that's how unthreatening he was. She was disappointed by the ferrets just now for being what they're made to be: wild.

As the cold pushes up through her shoes, lifting her, she relaxes. This is the same feeling she gets entering a bar or club. There are so many people, where else could she want to be? Everyone's here. She can relax and stop searching.

Last year at the fair, two kids were stabbed, one fatally. Sixteen undergrads ended the day in the hospital for alcohol poisoning. By Carla's supplemental statistics, about half the fairgoers lost their lunch, three quarters got too wasted to walk, and one million beer cans were crushed into silver pancakes on the pavement. The next day, sore and exhausted, she tried to peel one of these pancakes up, but it had fused with the road.

Kids sit on steps and drink, drawing boobs on their fore-heads, throwing a foam football so it wobbles on the yellow morning air. Some kids already hold their stomachs, bent over. Two girls fight, torsos leaning apart. No one pays attention to Carla. No one even knows they want to fuck her yet, won't know until they're halfway through. Though she's shivering in her pajamas under her coat, she needn't hurry. She lets her gaze settle on sinewy arms and beer bellies, breasts pushing at sweaters, chest hair poking from T-shirts, curly thick fuzz she could hold in her fist. A stirring builds low in her stomach.

A thick-bodied boy with a blond goatee passes, stumbling on smashed cans and stretching his arms out to steady himself. The kid doesn't look much like Dave, except for a quality of movement in the way he swings his arms, some echo in his loaf of solid hair. Her memories activate that easily, rehydrating like beans. She wants to grab the boy's padded waist, bury her nose in his shoulder and maneuver his penis into place.

"Hey," Carla calls, reaching out to grab his sleeve but stopping short, teasing.

The kid's pudgy face shines with questions. "Yeah?"

She laughs, harsh but easy, puffs of steam forming the shape of her mirth. "Sorry. I thought you were someone else." Her teeth ache in the cold.

"That's all right." The boy struggles to keep her here, an "um" buzzing under his breath. She bites her lip and walks away. She got him to notice her. That's her first step: plant the seed. Whether or not she encounters this particular boy later doesn't matter. The seed is for her. She has confidence, even in pajamas. She balances on the yellow line.

Carla and Dave met their senior year of college and dated for seven years. They were so in love that Carla hardly believes it now. Part of the problem was that she was a virgin when they met. She didn't know what a bad relationship was, so she couldn't appreciate a good one when it struck her in the face.

One weekend, in their last year together, Carla was out of town on behalf of the New York Public Library, at an MLA conference in Philadelphia. When she returned to their apartment, Dave was silent. He was usually such a talkative guy, heavy and rumpled, manipulating his doughy palms into endearing patterns while he spoke. So it was mystifying when he crashed on their futon for days, one leg on the rocking chair, socks dangling off his toes.

After work on the second day, she stationed herself in the threshold of their studio. "Dave. What the hell is going on?"

He combed a hand through his hair, leaving greasy tracks. "Something shitty happened. While you were away."

Carla was terrified, thinking Dave had been mugged, that they'd been evicted, that he had cancer. "What?"

"I got raped." He said it plainly, like he'd thought about it a lot, like this was definitely what had happened.

Carla wanted to laugh. Dave was over two fifty. No girl could rape him. But no—he must mean a man. Some hulking form pinning him in an alley in the East Village. She hated herself for this later but she thought about anal warts, rectal tearing, HIV. "Oh, Jesus," she said. She grabbed him into a hug, his slime of cold sweat breaking her heart.

When they separated, he said, "Remember how I went to Shane's party while you were gone?"

"Of course." She never got jealous of Dave going to parties

without her. First off, he was loyal, but second of all, Carla's attraction to him was singular.

"Well, I basically blacked out." That was typical Dave. Despite his size, his tolerance was low. He often woke her calling from the wrong ends of subway lines: Dyre Avenue, Van Cortlandt Park, Pelham Bay Parkway. "Babe," he'd say. "Where am I?"

"Okay," said Carla. "Then what?" At least they hadn't had sex since she'd been home. They might have to abstain for six months. She finds it ironic that she focused on that. She never worries about disease now and has never had a problem.

Dave sighed like this next part was impossible. But then he told her so clearly and easily that it was like he'd told other people already, his family and friends, strangers on the subway. He'd woken up in Shane's bedroom, lights on and the door half open, with a girl bouncing on him.

"Really?" Carla's first thought was surprise that a girl went after him. Then she filled in the scene. Shane was her friend too, had been since high school. That party was packed with her friends from all different circles.

"I shoved her off me," Dave said. "And ran."

He bowed his head into his hands and cried. Carla stroked his back, running her fingers in long, easy patterns. Dave didn't sound like a victim. Yeah, he was blacked out. But he'd probably been talking and awake and acting normal. They'd had whole conversations, whole subway rides, whole late-night trips to restaurants where he'd admitted afterward he was blacked out. Plus he'd fucked a girl with the door open. When she asked him more questions, the story got worse. The girl had cut her forehead when he pushed her off. And she was a younger cousin of Shane's.

Carla kept her ambivalence to herself. She was there for Dave during those next hard days. She cooked macaroni for him and called in sick for him and ascertained that his showers incorporated soap. She listened to him discuss the incident, recounting how, when he'd gained consciousness, he'd expected Carla. How he'd thought he'd recognized Carla's chubby cheeks and swinging ropes of hair.

For weeks Dave obsessed over the incident. He referenced it incessantly, especially whenever Carla had managed to forget. Then, one day, he returned to normal. He went back to work at the bar. He resumed drinking.

Carla snuck out to meet Shane at a diner, where she convinced him to convince the cousin not to present battery charges. The girl had needed minor plastic surgery.

"Dave's pretty upset too," she said, after Shane had railed at her for half an hour.

Shane screwed up his face. "Why?"

"He feels she took advantage of him." Carla couldn't say the word *rape*. Why couldn't she say it? She believed Dave. He'd blacked out. He'd never cheat on her. She drew a fork over her pancake, tearing the surface. "He was blacked out. He didn't consent."

Shane laughed, the wet cushion of his tongue pumping. "Come on, Carla. Jesus."

Her friends had talks with her, one by one, at brunches

that were designed to look casual but took U-turns into seriousness, plus one formal intervention where they said Dave had cheated on her and she had to admit it. They said she was in denial. She could forgive him or not but she had to start with the facts. She solemnly agreed because, at the time, part of her had believed that version too.

In the years after the relationship dissolved, when she was out every night sleeping with strangers, up late on Craigslist and OkCupid considering the bleak fluorescent-lit selfies of men and women slumped alone on couches all over the city—even messaging one guy whose profile picture was his pay stub—she hoped for another intervention.

Carla reaches the edge of the fair. Wind wraps her from three directions through the openings between buildings. The sharp air carries with it every other day in Madison: the short light, black ice, and lack of privacy. The color of Madison is slate blue—frozen lakes, concrete wedges of government offices and English departments, the snow churned up with beet juice and gravel. She turns and heads back into the fray. For half a block she closes her eyes, kids buffeting her from all sides, the smell of hormone stew. On this skinny strip of land between two lakes she's floating away from the rest of the country, alone.

When she opens her eyes at the end of the block, the action has thickened. Warmth pulses from kids all around. A boy's pants hang below his pubic hair. He pumps his hips in a pantomime of sex. Two girls vomit into the same puddle, giggling between heaves and pointing out curious bits. A boy rattles by with a backpack of bottles. Another kid drops a printout on a knife, demonstrating how sharp it is, but the printout slides off unharmed. The kid who died last year was only an extension school student, so the university didn't have to care. One email alert, and that was it. All the ghastly events of Madison are treated with Midwestern good cheer. Like in the sixties there was a slasher who'd visit Carla's library, slice up a couple girls' arms, and leave. They never caught him. At work people tap you with plastic cutlery and yell, "Gotcha!"

Carla takes in the sights, not jumping any guys yet. She's working up an appetite. The longer she delays, the hotter she burns, postponing pleasure, seeking her target. When she holds off longest, she goes the most wild.

Every house on Mifflin is open to a party. Kids move into places on this street just for today. Boys do keg stands on porches, play beer pong on roofs, laughing and screaming, cheeks wind-burned. A few limp by, bleeding. One from the nose, one from the lip, one from the elbow, one from the eye. The blood is shocking against drab jackets and gray jeans. Carla should be in a waterpark now, resting on a tube in a lazy river.

Carla never told Dave about her conversations with Shane or the intervention. She let them float apart, farther and farther, until she announced she was moving in with a friend. There was no official breakup. She said she needed space. She slept with other guys and Dave found out and retreated. He never chased her down.

As Carla crosses Broom Street and passes her apartment, a lone woman in the sea of boys sticks out as familiar. She's older than Carla, with faded orange hair. She talks to two kids in frosh-pride sweatpants. "I think you've got a great plan there, Raymond," she tells one boy, a redhead whose vertebrae poke through his shirt.

Both boys are underdressed in matching UW T-shirts, both sport mottled purple arms. Carla pictures them clinging to her and groaning, one per side. Her knees droop. The boys are younger than she usually lets herself like. Lately, the young ones appeal most. They're so far from pain.

"You'll go out and achieve your goals," says the woman. "It's healthy to have goals."

Carla slows as she passes, working out how she knows that scratchy voice. It's her sponsor, Shawna. Carla didn't even recognize her. How pathetic.

"Carla!" Shawna yells, churning her arm on the thin blue air.

Shawna reels Carla into a lung-crushing hug. "Hi," Carla says, voice muffled against Shawna's breasts. Shawna finally releases her grip. Carla pulls her coat closed, hoping Shawna didn't feel she's not wearing a bra.

"Meet Eddie and Christof." Shawna adjusts Eddie's hat, flapping up the brim. "Run along now, kids."

Shawna watches them leave.

"Is that your son?" Carla asks, not sure which kid she's referencing. Neither looks particularly like Shawna. But no one young would.

"Yup." Shawna hooks her arm into Carla's. "Shall we walk?"

"I guess." Carla can't say no, though Shawna scares her. Besides, if she goes the other way she has just that final block, and kids are bleeding over there.

"How does today look for you, personally?" Shawna asks.

"Okay," says Carla. "Just going to work. I might be late, actually." She speeds up as they cross a side street.

Shawna shakes her head. "Honey, I'm your sponsor. There is no reason at all to lie."

Shawna can't know Carla's schedule at the library, which changes weekly. "I do have work."

Shawna stops short, spins Carla around to face her. Behind Shawna's body, a few big guys softly toss a littler kid through the air. The kid flaps his elbows like he'll take off into the cold sky, leave this chaos behind. "Your friend had a talk with me this morning. She's worried about you today. She said you deserve a guardian angel."

Carla has laughed to Pooja about Shawna. Pooja agreed she sounded nuts, but Carla didn't even share Shawna's name. She barely knows Shawna's phone number herself. Pooja must have done some digging. This touches Carla so deeply that she pinches her bottom lip to keep it steady. Pooja actually cares. She didn't only come up with some half-assed, unappealing plan for Carla to travel alone to the hysterical Dells, full of foam rubber crocodiles and upside-down houses and waterslides with floating bandages. She didn't just offer to spend all day in the Buzzman Reading Room so

84

Carla wouldn't have to walk down Mifflin Street. She actually bothered to get help.

"I'm okay," Carla says. "I think I'll go home now." She really thinks she will, though her body is less sure, her feet aimed at an especially battered party house.

"Good idea," says Shawna. "I'll walk you."

"That's not necessary." But Carla's grateful, though she doesn't enjoy Shawna's company. She can't imagine retreating into her quiet apartment alone, sitting back down, and doing what? Watching TV? Playing with the ferrets? The ferrets only cost her money and time. Her fingers still stink of bleach and they didn't even appreciate her work. She should take them back to the pet store the next time she gets waxed. Maybe their friend is waiting.

When they start walking, Carla's colder than she's felt all day, her coat rubbing bare skin. Snow falls, gray confetti spaced far apart. Carla draws the flaps of her coat together and hunches her shoulders.

Shawna relates legends of SLAA, pat morality tales. Jenna, with her compulsion for unprotected sex, who contracted AIDS and now presents a lecture at middle schools called "Selling Your Life for a Minute of Fun." Natalie, whose recovery was facilitated by a wise older sponsor who guided her onto the right path. Selena, whose five hundredth one-night stand was with a folk rock star who told her "You're better than this, girly girl."

"She'd heard it so many times," Shawna says. "But that time, for whatever reason, it clicked."

"Because he was famous," Carla says flatly.

Shawna shrugs. "It doesn't matter how it happens."

That sounds like a motto printed on a T-shirt in Comic Sans font. How has Shawna managed to pack in so many stories on this short stretch of Mifflin? They detour around the foxiest kids. Sometimes Shawna pauses to collect a beer can or a soggy hot dog bun or, once, a plastic gallon bag of what looks like human shit. This she lifts all the way to her face before dropping it in horror. It's fuzzed with snow, like mold.

When they reach Carla's doorstep she's relieved. Soon she'll be alone again. She's not afraid anymore. This walk has prepared her. She'll drink tea. She'll call the pet store. She'll look out the window and watch for as long as she can. And then she'll go out later. Evening will be impossible to resist. But she'll keep her numbers down by starting late. "It was nice seeing you, Shawna."

"There's one more story, though." Shawna rubs a patch of dry skin on her jaw. "Do you have a minute?"

Carla nods. She can't be too rude. She needs to protect the outlet of the meetings. She'll recover soon enough, even if she relapses today.

"Remember the boys we just saw?" Shawna asks.

The red hair stuck out from behind the ears of one, the broad blond face of the other. Both boys looked encased in a skin of ice, like they'd walked the Wisconsin streets for months, like they'd never enjoy relief from the cold.

"They're not my kids."

This news is no surprise. Though Shawna is an authority

in the SLAA community, she has a dangerous edge. Like even if Carla trusted her with her sobriety, she'd never ask her to house-sit. She can't walk straight. Her lips never fully blanket her teeth.

"I used to do things with those boys," Shawna says. "When they were younger."

Carla can't imagine the kids any younger than they are now. They look like they just stepped into existence, their skin shiny and puffy, never yet sunburned or pimpled or bruised.

Shawna blinks, but snow clings to her eyelashes. She's about to explain what she did to those kids, who might be representatives from a larger group or maybe are her entire victim population. Either way it's horrible. She had sex with them or gave them drugs. Such stories are referenced every week at SLAA, though graphic details are discouraged. But maybe Shawna's story is even worse than the others. Maybe the highest ranked have committed the darkest actions. Maybe she made the boys fuck while she watched, or dressed them like babies. Maybe she had sex with them before they were of age, which is eighteen in Wisconsin. That was one of the first facts Carla checked when she moved.

What happened doesn't matter. Carla will hear the story, and she'll see her future in the jowls sagging around Shawna's mouth, in the words containing a sickening flavor of pride. "That's okay," Carla says. "I'm good." She opens her door.

Shawna dusts off her pants. "Let me come in for a coffee."

"You should go."

Before Shawna opens her mouth, Carla closes the door on the woman's wild hair, the skin sinking around her lips.

Inside, Carla leans against the door, exhausted. She's proud of saying no. She so rarely can. The snow is heavier now, though the sky is blue. She pulls down the venetian blinds. Buttery stripes of sunlight fall in line on the carpet. She'll pretend, for as long as she can fool herself, that it's nighttime, that the Mifflin Street Fair is over, that the undergraduates are safe in their beds, having escaped her tonight.

An unsettling feeling slides through her. Her apartment is too quiet. She approaches the ferret's cage, bumping her hips against furniture, hissing swears. Usually the ferrets are shifting against each other, walking on the wires, making their muffled chirp. There's enough light to discern a bulge in the pocket of their hammock, but why are they asleep? Her return always wakes them.

She loses her balance in the dark and braces herself against the cage. The bleach bottle sits by the door. She must have gotten it into their food bowl, or on the metal pipe of their water bottle. Or maybe they rubbed their humpbacks against the cage and then groomed themselves.

A chill slithers under her skin. She rips open the door and reaches into the fleece sleeve of the hammock. Her fingers meet warm bodies. She pulls them out, a ferret in each fist. They're groggy and limp but alive. She wants to leap into the air. That's when the smell reaches her: sweet and sticky. The newly cleaned litter box is splashed with waste, splotches coat the bars and the plastic ball. There's fluid everywhere. They must've evacuated their entire bowels. She barely gets them out before she throws up on the wall-to-wall carpeting. She forces her shaky body upright and carries the ferrets to the couch, where she lays them down.

There they lie, still and stretched out, the seams on their bellies rising only with labor. Her own breath stops. Her charges, her little sweeties. She needs their wiggly noses reanimated, needs to chase them under the bed and into the trash can. She can't be alone. All her progress will be reversed if she kills her own ferrets.

She squats and examines their frosted eyes. Any sickness in a creature so small must be fatal. Animals gather all their energy to hide symptoms. They're beautiful, lying there, their fur luminous. She genuinely loves them. She's never truly loved them before. She knows that now.

She fills a ramekin to the brim with water. She sets it on the couch and lifts weasel chins to the meniscus. The ferrets nose around, water beading on whiskered snouts. In unison, they drink greedily, dark spots pooling on the couch as they bury their faces as deep as they can, as though tastier reserves lie lower.

Pink tabs of tongue pop from furry chins. As water fills their long bodies, their coats grow shinier, their eyes brighter. Warmth glows in Carla. She'll do better for them from now on. She'll give them the care they deserve. She snuggles into the back of the couch. Maybe she'll tell Pooja about Dave after all. Maybe Pooja will affirm that Carla did her best in the situation, so she can finally let it rest. She lifts Boo high into the air. His head wags loosely. When he reaches her face, he opens his mouth. He'll bite if she draws him closer.

Pioneer

THE OREGON TRAIL RAN FROM THE BACK ENTRANCE
of Bridge Elementary down through the school yard to the
edge of the woods. Cones marked the journey. Not the satisfying soft cones that squish down with your body weight,
but hard plastic cones, prim and pointed as shark teeth. The
cones looped around the tree line to the right, and that's all
Coco and the rest of the Culver family could see from the
starting point. Who knew where the trail went after that?
There were dangers, Coco had heard, though she didn't
know exactly what.

When Ms. Harper had passed out the simulation's
rainbow-coded biography cards last week, Coco had not been
assigned to the Culver family. Her lemon-yellow card listed
her as the matriarch of the Bell family, who had lived right
here in historic Lexington, Massachusetts. Coco couldn't
bear to be a matriarch. While the class wandered around collecting their families, Coco asked Devon, the Bell patriarch,
if she could be a child in the Bell family instead.

"We already have two children," Devon said. "And there
can't be children without a matriarch."

"Sure there can," said Coco. "The matriarch could have died." They'd make up some woman who'd long since perished. Recalling her benevolence could pass the time on the trail.

"You want to be dead?" asked Devon.

"No," Coco said. "I just don't want to be the Bell matriarch. I want to be a Bell child."

"Why?"

Coco wouldn't say so to Devon, but she was uneasy in dresses and skirts. The wind could catch the fabric and expose the part of her she hated most, that felt so wrong and that she pretended had withered off her. In the role of a child, she'd be an eighteen hundreds tomboy. As matriarch there was no option. She'd have to look like a full woman. Ever since Coco's body had started developing a few months ago, she focused hard on the mildew on the ceiling while she washed herself, in order to forget her body. Only when the water was dirtied and lathered with soap could she bear to look down.

"I don't have the right clothes," she said.

"Ms. Harper said the girls could staple a sheet," Devon said. "A long sheet. Like touching the ground."

"Won't it get dirty?" Coco pictured herself as a bedraggled angel.

Devon shrugged.

At first Coco considered not traveling the Oregon Trail at all. She'd never played sick before, and that seemed like the type of trick every kid should pull once. But missing the day would be a crazy move. Coco loved Ms. Harper and would never lie to her. But beyond that, the Oregon Trail was the culmination of the fifth graders' hard work through Bridge Elementary, where you got to be a pioneer like those who'd traipsed around Plymouth Rock. Her classmates had chattered about the day since kindergarten, when they'd first glimpsed the wagons pulled through the field by what looked like small adults. All through middle and high school, the Oregon Trail would be reminisced about as the pinnacle of their education.

The day before the Oregon Trail, Coco asked the other families in Ms. Harper's class if she could join up with them. "Do you need a baby?" she asked the Murdochs and the Hancocks, the Bakers and the Blackthorns. "Or an adolescent?"

"No," they said, if they bothered with her at all. Even though it was still regular school until tomorrow, the families were already insular and protective, clumping around desks between subjects.

"Aren't you a matriarch yourself?" the Blackthorn matriarch asked.

"I don't want to be," said Coco. "I want to be a kid."

"That's stupid. Ms. Harper says we have to accept our station."

"Yeah," said the Blackthorn son, who blew his nose on his math worksheets. "Matriarchy is an incredible honor. Women rule."

"Want to trade?" Coco asked.

"Doy, no."

None of the girls assigned as daughters were interested in becoming matriarchs. Or at least they wouldn't admit it to Coco. The best option was to join the Culver family, who offered her the role of an ox.

"You can pull our wagon," said Alex, the Culver family patriarch. "If you can find another ox, we'll yoke you. It'll be super."

What she wanted to be was a boy. Like Devon or Alex, but nice. She wanted to wear short pants and follow behind a party, providing for anyone who was hungry. She wanted to be a smooth-faced, short-haired colonial boy.

At home that night, Coco stuffed yellow felt triangles with dry grass for horns and affixed them to the cap of her headgear. She prepared a poncho that simulated the powerful shoulders of an animal and tied a piece of rope to her belt for a tail.

"Coco," her mom said. "I thought you were a matriarch?"

Lately Coco hated the sound of her own name, which was like a pet's name or the name of a girl with makeup in a Western saloon, embarrassingly girlish, the verbal equivalent of balloons stapled to her chest. She twitched like she'd been hit. "I used to be."

"You look . . . You look like . . . I don't want to say it."

"What?" Coco struggled to speak clearly. Although her headgear was for night use only, she'd hooked the mouthpiece into the metal tubes on her molars. Otherwise the cap didn't stay taut on her head. "What do I look like?"

Her horns flopped over her eyes. Her mom didn't answer.

•

The next day, all four fifth-grade classes lined up at the head of the Oregon Trail. Each class was divided into six families of three or four members. People were meticulously dressed. The matriarchs wore full hoopskirts and aprons, bonnets and bodices with puffy sleeves, colonial dirt rubbed purposefully on the hemlines. The fathers and uncles wore leather vests and hats; the boys wore britches. The families pulled red wagons and garden carts and wheelbarrows to which they'd attached hula hoops with sheets over them, like genuine covered wagons. Everyone must have been gathering materials since kindergarten.

Coco snuck between the families in Mr. Bennett's class and Ms. Goldberg's class and Mrs. Hedgerow's class. Everyone stared.

"Are you a dog?" someone asked. "With headgear?"

"Are you an alien?"

"You look gay," said Devon, the Bell patriarch, who stood with a Radio Flyer and two motherless children.

"What do you mean?" Coco asked.

"Like a gay person? Ever heard of one? They're actually real. It's sick." He chuckled to himself. "See? Every girl here's wearing a dress. Even the daughters." He whipped his arm around to indicate the flapping sheets and costume dresses.

"So?"

"You're wearing stretch pants and a poncho and ears."

"I'm an ox." She sounded proud, as though the role were her idea.

"An ox?" one of her ex-children said.

Coco's ex-children were Peter and Marley. Peter was pale and smelled like the sawdust the janitors threw down when someone was sick on the floor. But Marley was actually popular. Why hadn't she stepped into the role of matriarch?

Last week, Marley had said Coco was chubby and stupid. That the headgear tubes on her molars poked into her cheeks and made her look part robot. Marley accosted Coco at the water fountain with a mechanical voice: "Ro-bot Co-co is a big fat dumbbell." Peter orbited Coco in a separate sphere. While Coco tried, and failed, to make friends with whomever she could hook, Peter was satisfied alone. Whenever she talked to him he smiled the wan smile of a beleaguered businessman and nodded.

"It's just," Coco said, "I'd rather be an ox."

She found the Culver family at the end of the row. The Culver patriarch, Alex, stood with the Culver matriarch, Victoria, before a loaded plastic wheelbarrow. They had no children but still preferred Coco as their ox.

"Where are your rations?" Alex asked, indicating the bed of the wheelbarrow, which was filled with baskets. The baskets held naked loaves of supermarket bread, unshucked ears of corn, plastic containers of dry oatmeal. "I expect every member of the Culver family to contribute to our stock."

"I brought flour," said Victoria, who wasn't the smiling

type. She wore a dark dress and a bonnet cinched around her face.

"Sorry," said Coco. "I didn't know oxen fed their families in colonial times."

Alex glared and passed her the handles of the wheelbarrow. "I can see we need to break you."

Mr. Bennett's class and Ms. Goldberg's class filed down the trail. The Culver family marched. The wheelbarrow, full as it was of grain, was exceedingly heavy. Coco had to rest the handles on her back and hunch over so she was nearly crawling. Other families, none of whom had oxen, shared the burden of their wagons and wheelbarrows. No one else had rations. Alex swallowed handfuls of oatmeal and hunks of bread as he walked. Coco only hoped he'd keep at it and lighten the load.

Halfway to the woods, the weight of the wheelbarrow increased significantly, and Coco dropped to her knees in the grass.

"Mush!" Victoria cried from her new position atop the wheelbarrow. Coco pushed back up to her feet and braced to bear her new load.

The first official obstacle on the Oregon Trail was disease. They arrived at a sign shaped like a gravestone that read DISEASE. A ghost popped up from behind the sign.

"I am the Spirit of Multiple Diseases," said the ghost.

Some of the families screamed. But it was obvious from the Long Island accent and red plastic glasses worn over the eyeholes in the sheet that the Spirit of Multiple Diseases was Ms. Goldberg. She pointed a long finger at random family members.

"Dysentery," she said. "Yellow fever. Dysentery. Scarlet fever. Yellow fever. Scarlet fever. Dysentery."

The chosen family members grabbed their hearts. Both Bell children were picked for yellow fever. Coco was given scarlet fever. Victoria, in the wheelbarrow, was selected for dysentery.

"Now," Ms. Goldberg said. "If your name starts with a letter between *A* and *E*, your disease is mild. You survive to live another day. Congratulations."

Shrieks of laughter and manic clapping rose among the mild sufferers. Coco's heart lifted, though she didn't join the cheers.

"If your first name begins with *F* to *O*, your disease is moderate. You live."

The group of moderates included Coco's ex-child Marley. She and the other moderate sufferers celebrated.

"Ah," said Ms. Goldberg. "But wait. You live, but unlike the mild sufferers, you do not escape unscathed. For the remainder of the journey, you must march with one leg dragging. The choice of leg is up to you, but it must always be behind you."

Marley said, "That's bull!"

"And now for *P* to *Z*," said Ms. Goldberg. "Are you children prepared for your fate?"

"Oh God," moaned Victoria from the wheelbarrow. "I don't want to limp all day in the sun."

Victoria wouldn't be doing much limping, perched as she was on the rations. Even if both her feet were struck down, Coco would keep yanking her along.

"Severe sufferers," Ms. Goldberg said. "You are dead. Please step forward."

Victoria deserted the wheelbarrow, lightening the load so fast that Coco's back snapped straight. Coco's ex-child Peter also marched forward, along with several other sufferers. They stood before Ms. Goldberg.

"Join your mass grave."

The severe sufferers lay down in front of the gravestone sign, the bottoms of their feet wagging at the survivors. Coco tried not to rejoice at their fate. Smiling with her headgear hurt, anyway.

"March on, brave pioneers," Ms. Goldberg said to the remaining party. "But march with heavy hearts."

The Oregon Trail wound down to the rim of the woodlands. There the party turned and marched along the tree line. Past the monkey bars and swing set, a creek cut through the playground. The creek was three inches deep, and children were forever damming it up, opposed, for some reason, to its free flow. Full of rocks and pine needles, the creek was rendered even shallower than its already pathetic potential. But still, parents rallied against it, claiming children could drown in an inch of water. Coco had squatted at the creek before, placing her face as close as possible to the surface. Thin water slid over mud, blurring her vision. All she'd have to do was push her nose in.

Mrs. Hedgerow appeared at the other side of the creek. "Halt, party." Her breasts and stomach bubbled under a garment of blue rubber. She'd stapled toy fish to her outfit like a kind of Mother River.

"Kudos," Mrs. Hedgerow said. "You have reached the Goodstone Waterway."

"That's just the creek," Alex said. "Big whoop."

"It is a giant whoop, young man," Mrs. Hedgerow said. "For you must manage a crossing."

"I know how to cross it," said Alex. "That's so easy it's stupid."

He leaped onto the wheelbarrow. Coco was ready this time and didn't fall.

"Mush!" called Alex. "Mush, ox!"

Coco stiffened. The whole living fifth-grade class watched. She hated when people stared. They must see something she couldn't, and the attention itched. Even so, she set her feet in the Goodstone Waterway and dragged Alex and the rations to shore. Once safely across, she rotated the wheelbarrow to face her classmates, careful not to feel pride. All she had done was what Alex had forced her to do. From behind her he tossed a wedge of bread at the unlucky souls on the far shore. The chunk landed in the creek, swelling below the surface like a hunk of flesh.

"Mr. Culver, please settle down," said Mrs. Hedgerow. "Remember, you are a pillar of this community."

"I am?" asked Alex.

"Consult your biography card, young man, and you will find you are a member of the local council and a well-respected truth teller."

None of the fifth graders had read their biography cards. They were too hard. All Coco had managed of hers was "Eleanor Bell is a most curious and intriguing lady of the middling fiscal class" before she gave up.

"I regret to say that Mr. Culver has indeed chosen a legitimate route across the Goodstone Waterway. I did not know you children were issued oxen this year. Anyone else in possession of an ox may step forward at this time."

No one did, so Mrs. Hedgerow gave the signal for the crossing to continue. She narrated the travails of each family. Whole parties were sent back halfway through after their wagons buckled and their families drowned. The Blackthorn son was sucked dry by leeches. The Murdoch patriarch contracted giardia and perished when he was already on the other side, observing the Baker family crossing. Certain individuals were singled out as drowners, like Coco's ex-child Marley.

"Your limp handicapped you," Mrs. Hedgerow said.

"Well, duh," said Marley.

"I mean to say it killed you."

By the end of the crossing Mrs. Hedgerow had killed thirty additional family members. She herded them off and left the depleted party to continue on.

Each family had lost at least one member. The peace of the insular groups had snapped and now they had to function as an unwieldy whole. Coco didn't know if they could manage. Maybe, for the first time in the history of Bridge Elementary, the pioneers would fail.

Alex stood up on the wheelbarrow, which waggled painfully in Coco's grip, the weight shifting as he sought balance.

"Forward, party," he said. "We must press on."

The families lined up behind Alex and Coco. Now that Alex was exposed as an ox-owning pillar of the community, the party was eager to follow him.

Past the creek was a multipurpose field. Over the years, Coco had uncovered baby turtles in the field, a nest of condoms, a gold ring. The grass was long. You could find anything in it.

"Keep to the tree line for cover," said Alex, though the orange cones ran a haywire path through the center of the field.

The families hadn't gone two hundred feet past the creek when Mr. Bennett jumped from the forest directly in front of the Culver family wagon. He wore grease paint smeared up his cheeks, a suede coat with jangling tassels, and a cardboard headband with stapled feathers. The feathers were each a foot long, the most vibrant blues and yellows and scarlets. If they were real they would have been exceedingly valuable due to their size and color, but Coco recognized them immediately as craft feathers. Virtually worthless.

"You're under attack," Mr. Bennett announced.

"Who would dare attack us?" asked Alex.

"The Feather Weather tribe," said Mr. Bennett.

Alex's face twisted angrily. "Ha. Who is it, Ms. Harper?"

Mr. Bennett grinned as dead family members poured from between the trees. Each dead pioneer had their own headband and their own feather. As they advanced, they stirred up the pine scent of the forest. There were more of them than there were living pioneers. And they were armed.

Every member of the Feather Weather tribe carried a homemade bow fashioned from a stick and a string. The bows were serviceable for shooting kindling, though their power was dubious. Victoria led the pack, her face obscured by inelegant swaths of paint.

"Die, die!" she cried, shooting kindling from her bow.

"Anyone struck in the chest is considered dead," said Mr. Bennett.

The tribe poured among the pioneers. Kindling bounced off their chests and backs. Coco dropped to four legs. Alex tumbled off the wheelbarrow and rolled underneath. The crippled sufferers were felled first. Some pioneers leaped in front of the arrows, perhaps preferring to join the exciting band.

Coco prayed she wouldn't be shot. She needed to complete the trail. Between bobbing feathers and twigs hurtling through the sky, she peered west across the school yard. She was a true pioneer, one ocean behind her and another—one she'd never seen and might never reach—ahead. She didn't want regular school to resume. She wanted to survive, to stay in the game.

Mr. Bennett dragged the corpses out of danger. Victoria pillaged the Culver family wagon, munching through loaves of bread and shoveling dry tapioca and Wheatena into her mouth.

Marley and Peter, Coco's ex-children, surrounded her.

"So you won't be our mother?" asked Marley, aiming a sharpened twig at Coco's underbelly. "You're too good for us, huh?"

"Yeah. Huh?" asked Peter.

"You'd rather be livestock than our mother, huh? You'd rather be on your hands and knees and, like, pooping in the grass, huh?"

Marley's eyes were wet as she stuttered out *huh* after *huh*. Like she was genuinely asking, *Will you be our mother? Why aren't you our mother?* But Marley thought Coco was a fat, stupid robot.

Coco flattened down so her chest met the grass and no one could strike her. She stuck her nose in the dirt, facing a smudge of brown. A twig landed on her back so lightly it was loving. She'd survive, no matter what.

When the massacre ended, all but a handful of pioneers had died. Alex was alive, having evaded the tribe under a wagon. Devon, the Bell patriarch, was also alive, as were a few scattered matriarchs and patriarchs. All the children were dead.

The band met in the center of the field, which was littered with arrows. Only seven pioneers remained.

"How far do we have left?" asked Coco.

"Shut up, ox," said Alex. "Oxen don't discuss."

Coco shielded her eyes from the sun. The path swung through a patch of milkweed around to the front of the school. The markers were farther apart the longer you traveled the Oregon Trail. The teachers must've run low on cones.

"We need rations," the Blackthorn matriarch said. "We're starving."

"Get your rations then," said Alex.

"We don't have any," said the Blackthorn matriarch.

"Yeah," said a kid in another class. "We don't got none."

"Well, you can't have ours." Alex turned to Coco. "Ox, guard the rations."

"But they're hungry." Coco didn't get what the big deal was. She wasn't hungry, but if other pioneers were, they should eat. The Culvers had so much food, albeit dry, flavorless food.

"No," said Alex. "They're fine."

"We're hungry," said the Blackthorn family matriarch.

"We're hungry," said Devon.

Devon and the Blackthorn matriarch approached the Culver family wagon. "We're hungry," they chanted. "We're hungry, hungry, hungry." The other living party members joined the chant.

"Wait," said Coco. "We'll never eat all this." Devon and the Blackthorn matriarch had been nasty to her in the past, but so had almost everyone at Bridge at some point. Coco tore off a chunk of loaf and held it out to Devon, who jammed it in his mouth. Alex grabbed Coco's wrist.

"That's Culver family food," he said. "Not ox food. Not community food."

Alex twisted Coco's wrist as if to snap it off her body and throw it into the wagon for an extra ration.

"You're gay," he said. He smirked at Devon and they laughed.

"I know, right?" said Devon.

"You're worse than gay," Alex said. "You're not even a person. You're an ugly ox with ox balls. You're a gross animal."

The party chanted, "An-i-mal, an-i-mal." Coco backed up against the wagon as they approached.

Gripping the bread as a shield, Coco wondered if she actually was an animal. That explained why she didn't feel like anyone else at school. She certainly wasn't normal.

The party closed in. Kids held rocks above their heads, the broken handle of a wagon, a bent length of hula hoop, a torn sheet flapping in the air. "An-i-mal," they said. "An-i-mal."

But Coco hadn't chosen to be an ox. If she'd been allowed to be a boy on the Oregon Trail, everything would have worked out. With all the funny costumes, the marshmallow wagons and false names, maybe her new look would've escaped notice. She'd change slowly after that. A baseball cap, a haircut, a nickname.

Devon's fingertips reached Coco's chest. She screamed. The scream wasn't a kid's scream or a pioneer's scream. It was wild and wet and injured. Like something you'd hear in the backwoods, but only from a distance.

Devon retreated on the lawn. "What's your problem?" Alex asked, sounding like he didn't want to know.

Then someone behind them said, "Greetings, party." The moment she spoke, in that voice that could have been set to music, Coco recognized Ms. Harper. The pioneers turned to face this final spirit.

"I am the Spirit of Personal Dissonance," Ms. Harper said, from under her wave of crispy silver hair.

The Blackthorn matriarch backed up, spilling fistfuls of flour like snow over the feet of the surviving party.

"Doesn't sound scary," Alex said. "Don't even know what that is."

"Well," said Ms. Harper. "I'm surprised you don't know what dissonance is, because you, young man, are the cause of it."

"But I'm a pillar of this community," said Alex.

"Not anymore." Ms. Harper twirled a twig in Alex's face. "Lie down. You were shot with a musket by the Bell patriarch."

"Ha," said Devon. "Gotcha."

"Alas," said Ms. Harper. "Not before the Bell patriarch was mortally wounded by the Blackthorn matriarch's bayonet, which she then, in misery, turned on herself."

Ms. Harper narrated the deaths of three pioneers from

another class. That was the last of them; six pioneers slumped in the clover with their eyes shut.

"I'm not ready to die," Coco said.

"It's all right, Coco," said Ms. Harper. "You don't die."

Winning was this easy. But she wasn't even proud. She took a breath. "That's not my name anymore."

Ms. Harper looked confused, but soon her expression settled. "The game's over, honey." She set her hand on Coco's spine to guide her back to school.

Really, the end of the simulation was just the beginning. Coco knew that now. Not even Ms. Harper could help her. She pulled away and turned to face the yellow field, the milkweed, the curved path of cones. The sun was a low white hole in the sky. She would go on her journey now. She would set off.

Counselor of My Heart

AFTER CROSSING MEMORIAL DRIVE ONTO THE BANKS of the Charles, Molly let her quasi-girlfriend's dog off the leash. Chowder bounded next to her, limbs flapping against the snow, so puppyish she wanted to shove him over. But nothing could annoy her now, not even this brat. She had a day off from the hot dog stand. The air smelled like fire.

She was just wishing the dog away when she became half-aware of the squirrel skittering across the frozen river, the scrape of its claws like a rake dragged over plastic. Later she'd wonder why she didn't turn and face the squirrel, seriously question his purpose on the ice. Did he think he'd buried a nut out there? *Had he, actually?* Was it floating, swollen, an inch above the river bottom?

Chowder took his time noticing. He was a foolish dog, though German shepherds are famously bright. Perhaps the white ones like Chowder, rabbity and smiling, had been bleached of their smarts. Beth, who Molly was dating, had owned Chowder for ten years. Ten frustrating years, probably, though Molly had only met Beth last February. She pictured the rodenty puppy he must've been, the birthday cakes he'd flattened, the urine sprinkled on carpets like holy water.

When Chowder saw the squirrel, he didn't stop to point or stare, judge distance or probability of success. He tore off across the frosty grass and rinds of stale snow and slipped down the bank onto the river. He turned wild for a second, properly vicious. His hackles rose, his tail flagged, his teeth golden against his white coat. Even when his paws slipped, they slipped together, all four at once, propelling him farther and faster across the ice.

Just as Chowder was an inch from seizing the squirrel, thunder sounded and the ice gave way. The squirrel vanished into the rip without disturbing the river, and Chowder followed, faithful to the chase, pitching nose first into the mouth of charcoal water.

For a heartbeat, his tail stuck out, whiter than the ice or the overcast sky. Molly wondered if anyone was watching from the Weeks Footbridge or the Lowell Towers or that mysterious factory across the river. But then Chowder was gone and the squirrel was gone and Molly was still standing on the bank. She hadn't taken a step.

There was a hole in the river now. A gray-blue shadow that couldn't be big enough to swallow a chihuahua, much less a shepherd and a squirrel. Molly watched the hole for longer than any mammal's lung capacity before she realized she should move, take action.

She hurried to the water's edge and slammed her foot on the ice. Her sneaker swam around like crazy—ice was slippery, of course. She couldn't cross it. She wished she had skates. Could she rent skates quickly, or steal some off a kid? She paced the bank, scanning for a sturdier path of ice to the hole. She called Chowder's name until her voice gave out, straining for an answering splash.

Leaving felt wrong, but what else could she do? Walking back through Harvard Square, shaky with uncertainty that what had happened was real, her steps unsteady on the flagstones, the leash grew heavy around her neck. She was balling it up to stick in her bag when a kid in a VERITAS = BEER sweatshirt said, "All you need is a dog!"

A shot of acid struck Molly's throat. "Are you volunteering?" She restrained herself from slapping his fat prodigy cheeks.

She returned to Hurlbut Hall, commonly known as Pukeass, to the first-floor suite where Beth was a tutor. Beth was away for last night and all of today, presenting a paper in Delaware, and had asked Molly to stay with Chowder. Harvard tutors were allowed to have pets on the first floor. Beth said that was because the dogs exited quickly without sloughing dandruff on the stairs and halls. Some of the students on the upper floors had sensitivities.

"You mean allergies?" Molly was surprised they let a dog in the dorms at all.

"No," said Beth. "If there were allergies I wouldn't be in Hurlbut. But some of the students are sensitive."

That was an understatement. The Harvard kids were at Beth's door from dawn until dawn again. There was never a free moment to crawl between the sheets without some wiener tapping that sharp knock that said, "While I acknowledge that, in theory, I'm a needy piece of crap, I nevertheless require your immediate response."

The freshmen wanted advice about applying to med school or to report that their neighbors' GChat alerts were turned up too loud or that the toilet seats were splashed in poop residue and the showerhead holes coated in gum. The gum was intended to increase water pressure but ended up steaming people in mint. Beth indulged the students like precious, dear children, nodding deeply at their monologues, tapping their shoulders and rolling her eyes at their pain.

Molly entered the suite. Every surface was layered with overlapping rugs and southwestern blankets, an effort to make a dorm cozy when you were in your late twenties and unwilling to surrender anymore to bluish institutional white.

When she sat on the armchair she felt, for an instant, the smiling muzzle of Chowder in her lap. This was the first time she'd sat here without him burrowing in, as though out of sweetness, and then taking a long drag of her crotch. Beth wasn't coming back until later tonight, but Molly should call and tell her what had happened. Beth loved Chowder more than she loved Molly, or her family, or herself, crazy as that was.

Molly listened to the ocean on the receiver before dialing out of the Harvard system and onto the sonic wave of tone. Beth was in session, or in the hotel revising. Her presentation was in an hour, and her phone was off. Molly cleared her throat, preparing to leave a message in her ghastliest voice. The news would land smoother when Beth called back expecting dire news.

But then, abruptly, Beth was on the line.

"I have to get dressed in two minutes," she said, as though they were already midconversation. "Judith Butler is here. I can't believe no one warned me. I have to raise the barn. I have to."

Beth bungled aphorisms, which Molly found endearing, considering she was in her fourth year of a Comp Lit PhD. She'd finished her coursework but couldn't begin her dissertation until she accumulated three first-author publications. She was presenting a paper at a conference called Bodies that Matter.

"Then raise the barn," Molly said. She normally hated discussing Beth's stress, which washed over her like secondhand smoke, reminding her of all the careers she wasn't pursuing, all the progress she wasn't making. But right now she'd take any topic but Chowder.

"How am I supposed to raise the barn if I've been writing this paper for three months and I've already raised the goddamn barn a thousand times, like off the farm and practically out of the atmosphere, and now I can't raise it any higher or everything's going to topple like some kind of, I don't know, tower of scarves? Cars? Whatever that's called?"

Molly pictured a soft, wobbling skyscraper, bright with knitted stripes. Far more inviting than dreary playing cards. Beth's versions were always better.

"I have an hour, Molly. You never call."

The leash was coiled on the floor, spring-loaded, ready to strike. If Molly dumped the news on Beth now, she'd ruin the presentation. "I'll talk to you when you get home? Good luck."

"Okay. Kiss the beast."

A pang ripped through Molly. She should've told Beth. But she also shouldn't have let Chowder off leash. As long as she was wishing.

She leaned back in the armchair. She'd wait until the panel started, then leave a message. She tried to relax into the upholstery, tried to enjoy these last hours of calm, but she couldn't settle. There was Chowder's rawhide, his deflated teddy bear, his vulgar, bald tennis ball, all the toys that would never be squeezed or squished, thrown or caught, eaten or slurped on again. She gathered his possessions. She hid his bag of kibble under the sink, on top of the last inch of drooly water still in his bowl. In the highest cabinet she stuffed his squeaky T-bone steak and the last pack of Snausages. Into the toe of her boot went a disc of fur that had floated for weeks like a fuzzy flying saucer.

But she still couldn't relax. Ever since she was fifteen, she'd leaned on substances in times like this. The memories were enough to lighten her: NyQuil mixed with root beer, a huff of computer keyboard cleaner, cocaine, even if it had that grainy yellow look and was mostly lactose or baking soda. Even now that she was living the domestic life she needed a boost sometimes, though she hid the worst from

Beth. A couple glasses of wine usually did the trick, but alcohol was banned in freshman dorms. Fortunately Molly had a sandwich bag of pot for emergencies.

Beth let her smoke in the bathroom, the last room in the railroad suite, with her head out the window at night when no one was on Prospect. This seemed more incriminating than smoking inside and lighting a cranberry-scented candle afterwards, but Beth was more afraid of the little Harvard shits than the campus police or even the real police. Right now, though, it didn't matter. Molly had killed Beth's dog. She smoked right in the armchair

Molly's own apartment was in Allston. Across the river there were no rules or snotty students, but she had five roommates, bedbugs, and rats. Not mice, but rats. Bulge-backed, two-pound goblins that dragged themselves across the floor without fear of humans. If you yelled or stomped they planted down and stared, as though saying, "You're sixty times my body weight and that's the best you can do?" Even so, she preferred her place to this womb of eighteen-year-olds. She was stuck with Beth in this dorm, too domestic. She was afraid of how much she liked just hanging out and having sex, watching TV, reading for the first time in years. Wasn't she too young to be this boring?

Ever since Molly had graduated from Northeastern four years ago she'd been working at the vegan hot dog stand and playing as many shows as possible at T.T.'s and the Lizard Lounge and sometimes, if she was lucky, Club Passim. She had a couple good songs, one about a tomboy riding the highline through Montana, another about coming out in fourth grade. She had some bad songs too, but she needed filler.

She first spotted Beth at one of her shows from her perch atop her rickety stool. She noticed Beth because she was older, heavier, and more fastidiously dressed than Molly's normal fan base. Large-bosomed and prim, Beth reminded Molly of a camp counselor at some camp she'd never attended, who was critical of the children but stood naked before them. Who taught them how to pull the udder of a cow with slipping, lubricated fingers and didn't realize how erotic it was. At twenty-seven, she was a virgin.

Molly referred to Beth among her regulars at the hot dog stand as Counselor of My Heart. Her lust inflated as she eased bobbing dogs from their boiling juices, painted ketchup on buns in the shape of wobbly lips. "She sounds perfect," businessmen and professors agreed as they chewed through tubes of soy. After five friend dates, Molly cornered Beth before a screening of *Happy Together* at the Brattle and kissed her. To Molly's surprise, the involvement escalated from there. Beth had definitely come close to saying she loved Molly the other day. Her eyes were glassy with nerves as she said she had to tell Molly something. Molly changed the subject fast. Beth couldn't love her, being so much smarter, so much more put together. Not dependent on substances. Not a failed musician.

Molly got viciously high. But no matter how high she got she was haunted by that pale tail sticking out of the ice, paws pedaling water thick with cold. She dug out her travel guitar, three-quarter sized, a gift from Beth, frankly higher quality than her main guitar. She warmed up on scales and picked out a new tune. Just A-D-A-D-A-D-C, plain as you can get. She tried to make it funny, to cheer herself. "Counselor of My Heart," she sang. "Counselor of My Heart, don't come home too soon. Counselor of My Heart, I hope your flight's delayed." Her throat was sore from screaming for Chowder.

As she wound down the first verse, there was a tight-fisted rap at the door. Molly extinguished the joint and kept playing. "Will you forgive me, Counselor of My Heart? Will you still sleep with me like you do so well?"

The rapping continued. The Harvard kids were so urgent. They even brushed their teeth urgently, specks of blood flinging onto the mirrors. They washed their faces until they shone like peeled beets. On their eyelids were fierce marks where they bore down too firmly with eyeliner pencils.

Molly composed one more verse: "Counselor of My Heart, will you survive today? Will you get a new dog, a smart dog, a graceful dog? Golden dogs, gorgeous dogs, sexy dogs, Harvard dogs?" before she had to admit the kid wasn't going away. She flicked the smoke to dilute it and pulled the door open an inch.

A boy stood in the fluorescent-lit hall. He had sandy hair and unfashionable glasses, flannel pants and a T-shirt that read GIVE BONE MARROW above a flexible, grinning femur. "Excuse me, ma'am," he said. "By chance has Beth Barrett yet returned?"

"No." Molly limited her interactions with students. If anyone said "Hi" to her in the hall, it was that "Hi, I have a question" voice, "Hi, I have ulterior motives. Hi, I want to take advantage of you really fast." Molly started to close the door.

"Wait," the boy said. "Who's on duty? The third-floor guy? There's a problem."

"There's no problem," Molly said. "Why don't you run along?"

"But it smells like marijuana. I think it's from 6A." The boy's glasses were so dense and uneven that his expression was unreadable. As he shifted, his eyes behind the lenses blurred and refocused. "Where's the dog?" he asked. "Beth said someone was staying with the dog."

Molly didn't like that *someone*. It sounded too much like *anyone*, even though she didn't call Beth her girlfriend yet, either, wasn't ready to have a real girlfriend. Like she wasn't ready to have a real job or a real music career, as though she had the option for either.

"I don't hear him," the boy said. "Chowder. Chowder."

Molly cracked the door wider. She didn't want the R.A. on the third floor hearing all this talk of drugs and dogs. The R.A. was only a junior himself and bleated to Beth about his parents' divorce, his homesickness, the soulless pursuit of Economics. "Come in," she said.

"Beth said I could walk Chowder anytime," he said, upon entering. "I want to walk him."

Molly slouched against the wall. There was a quality to

this kid that made her want to thoroughly disappoint him. "Now isn't a good time."

The boy was a slice shaved off a more substantial boy. He picked up the leash, hung it on his finger like a snakeskin, swinging. Molly remembered seeing him now, with Beth in the hall, cuddling the shepherd's big head, his fleece matted with fur. He was one of those kids with a dog back home who couldn't stand a life free of gamey aromas and feces handling.

"Sit down, please." Molly took the leash. "And stop groping things that don't belong to you." The Harvard kids, for all their intensity, just wanted to be treated like children. They relaxed when following orders.

Molly closed the door to Beth's bedroom, establishing the possibility that Chowder was somewhere in the suite, though the softest knock sent him rocketing to the door, woofing with his tongue out, ecstatic to meet whoever might emerge from beyond the wooden frame. Rapists and serial killers, he welcomed them all.

The boy sat down.

"Who are you?" he asked. "I've seen you."

"I'm Beth's, you know, person." Saying that out loud was awkward. Molly had never before admitted to an official relationship with Beth, or anyone for that matter. The fumbling sentence was out before she considered that perhaps Beth didn't want students knowing she was gay. Perhaps that was why "someone" was watching the dog. Of course, Molly was wearing a man's flannel and had shaggy hair. She was ever-present, and there was one bed.

The boy's eyes inflated. "Beth's, like, a gay lesbian?"

"Yup." In fact, Beth's sexuality wasn't official. She hadn't come out to her family or friends, though Molly had encouraged her with the gift of a T-shirt featuring a blasé-faced rainbow. Beth didn't even know the term *come out*, but said "come forth" as in, "Do you think Larry Summers will ever come forth from the closet?" Her gay-dar was also abysmal. But she acted gay enough. Molly had long thought the information should be public. And she'd always known she'd have to follow through while high. She relit the joint, watching the fleshy machine of the boy's brain kick into gear.

"You're smoking marijuana."

Molly wagged her eyebrows. "Sure about that, kid?"

"James," he said. Defiantly, he reached out his knobby hand for the joint.

She let him have it. Why not? Everything was shit now.

James took a drag.

"You don't have to hold it in for an hour."

He let the smoke leak out his nostrils, snorting at the burn. It was nice to share with someone for once. Beth never caved to a drag, even on her most anxious nights. "Pot makes me paranoid," she said. Or "Pot makes me stupid." It wasn't until she said "Pot makes me gassy" that Molly realized pot didn't make Beth anything because she'd never tried it.

James's eyes went pink and he slumped into the armchair, painting his pajamas with a full coat of dead dog hair. Why was he in pajamas at 6:00 p.m.? Because the Harvard students wore their pajamas all day, all over town: their genitals bouncing in sweatpants, their stomachs expanding against the forgiving pressure of elastic waists.

"So," James said. "Tell me. Where's the dog?"

Molly shouldn't say. Why would she, when he could use the information against her later? He was an entitled kid who couldn't sympathize with her position. But one of the symptoms of Molly's high was babbling. And once she started she always told the whole story.

She described Chowder jogging down the riverbank and how she'd been almost close enough to reach his brush of tail, if she'd only reacted quickly enough. She told the boy each shade of emotion she'd experienced: How at first the tail disappearing was funny, like a cartoon where the world broke open and pulled a silly wolf under its soft surface. How her next thought was relief. She actually considered that Chowder hadn't pooped yet, and now she wouldn't have to touch it. But then she thought of Beth, and a fist squeezed her heart.

"I didn't even fully step on the ice," Molly said.

"That would've been stupid," James said. "If he fell through, you obviously would have." He said it like he was answering an exam question, some calculation of body mass divided by structural stability, without consideration for feelings.

"I should've walked out a few steps. At least until it cracked. At least so I had."

James fingered his eyes until Molly couldn't tell if the resultant tears were from grief or physical pain. "Chowder, Jesus. What a dog."

"I know," said Molly, and now that Chowder was dead, she sort of meant it. All his dumb affection had value, probably.

"You must really love her," James said.

Molly smelled a trap, but she was curious. "Why do you say that?"

"You're crying over a dog."

"You're crying too." He was, though his streaming tears didn't dilute his rational tone.

"They're just dogs. He was sort of old, right? Dogs die. They just die. You know, at our farm? Dogs were always dying. We threw the extra litters into Canada."

"I thought you were from Greenwich, Connecticut." Everyone here was either from New York City or Greenwich, Connecticut.

"What? No. North Dakota." James struggled up in the chair, as though attempting a more dignified pose. He threw out an arm in a loose-jointed gesture. "The point is, they're animals. They do the best they can. Like people come here more for Chowder than Beth. He did his job, and now he's gone."

"Not naturally, though." Molly squeezed her eyes shut. She was hit with Chowder's claws scraping the river bottom, his eyes popping nerves.

"Still."

Molly was beyond high, out of her mind. She was in the sky above Prospect Street, watching the plain square of Hurlbut Hall. In the open air it was evident that Beth loved her with the most energy of anyone Molly had ever been with.

That Beth was the smartest person Molly had ever known, the most patient with Molly's flimsy musical career, her fake job. Who cared about her prudishness, her stress? Those features hardly mattered when you looked at the whole of their life together. "Yes, I do. Very much."

"Do what?" asked James.

Molly shook the hot idea from her head. "Never mind."

"We should distract you," James said. "Let's cook something."

"Like, what, spaghetti?" Molly subsisted on day-old hot dogs and hot dog accoutrements. A bowl of relish and cabbage shards was almost a salad. She topped it with a toxic yellow swirl of mustard.

"Like a cake, maybe." James jumped up and bounced on his heels.

"That's silly." But she liked the idea: Beth coming home to fresh cake, Molly acting, for once, all domestic and responsible.

They stirred together quantities of flour, sugar, Swiss Miss, maple syrup, mini marshmallows, frozen blueberries, and rice milk. They left the mixture lumpy, at James's insistence, to "preserve tenderness." They slid the cake into the oven with the heat all the way up, to bake it faster. They smoked again. They fell asleep in the armchairs.

When Molly woke, the door was already open and the smoke alarm was already screeching high, even wails through the clouded air. She might have slept through all that if Beth weren't shouting, "Are you okay? Molly?" Beth saying her name, even sharply, always got her. Molly sat up, stood up, stumbled, and fought for the kitchen through the smoke. Somehow, still high, she managed to turn off the oven and remove the battery in the alarm and open all the windows before she realized she was moving. Smoke alarms were familiar rivals.

The air thinned, and Molly squinted through it. James was still asleep in his chair and Beth was standing in the doorway in a dress shirt with her breasts pushing gaps between the buttons. She gripped a leather duffel. "Molly?" she said, uncertainly. "What's going on?"

"We forgot the cake," Molly said.

"Why is James Masterson here?" Beth looked at James like he was a weasel who'd crawled in under the door. A smell rose off her, the wrong kind of hormone.

"I'll get rid of him."

Molly had screwed up. Why was it her instinct to bury a mess with another mess? Once at a party she'd disguised a wine stain on a linen rug with a turned-over platter of deviled eggs. As soon as she forced her feet to move she shook James awake, his mouth spilling drool down his bone marrow shirt.

"Hi, girls," he said.

Beth stared at Molly like she didn't know her. Molly hoped it wasn't a relationship-ending stare. She suspected it was.

"Come on, James," Molly said. "Let's get you back to your room." She grabbed his arm, but it was limp.

"Oh, my murderer," he said. The words froze Molly's spine.

Molly flinched. "He's high," she said. "I'll walk him home." She propped James upright, but he couldn't stabilize. She passed Beth with the boy held out before her like a floppy shield.

Beth peered into his dazed face. "James?"

"Thank you for all you do. On behalf of all students. Sincerely." He saluted her, then relaxed against Molly's support, a deflating little Christ.

In the hallway, Molly propped him against a wall. "Are you really that high?" Usually White Kush didn't have a late-onset effect, but he might have "sensitivities."

"Did I do a good job?" His sandy hair flipped up. "I thought if I acted that bad I could pretend tomorrow I don't remember. And, like, get you out of trouble."

James had a point. If he'd been coherent Beth would've insisted on questioning him, and no one stood up to Beth's questions, not even Molly. "Why'd you call me a murderer?"

"Come on," he said. "You killed her dog."

Molly's arm twitched to hit him. He was an entitled brat like she'd suspected, meddling in her affairs without a blip of remorse. But she made herself breathe. Maybe he was right. She had to tell Beth about Chowder. Of course she did. That would be the first question when she reentered the suite. And now, an opening. *Why did James Masterson call you a murderer? Oh, that? Because I am one.* She should slap herself for failing to leave a voicemail while Beth was on her panel. At least James hadn't told Beth that Molly had outed her.

When she entered the suite, the cake was on the burners, Beth pushing smoke out the window with a rag. "What are you doing? Why was James here? Why is a cake burning in the oven? Why is the dog food under the sink? And where is the dog?"

The questions rushed at Molly, pricking her skin. Beth would find out any second what had happened. There were only a few moments left in her life where Chowder lived on. Molly covered her face against the assault. "I'm high."

"Great. I'll add that to the list of delightful events that occur when I leave for two days. You corrupt my students; you give them drugs. Jesus. I could lose my job." She held her hand to her mouth as if to block herself from saying more.

"I'm sorry." Saying the words was like eating an insubstantial snack, reminding you how hungry you are.

"Oh, great. That makes it all okay. All is solved now, because you're sorry."

That was it. Poor, idiotic Chowder at the bottom of the river. James Masterson's innocence, gone. Her relationship with Beth, ending tonight, just when Molly had decided it was what she wanted. And she couldn't change any of it. She leaned against the cold tiles and cried. She cried until she convulsed, until she had to run to the bedroom and lay on the quilt, the bed a mossy field beneath her, dragging her down. The tears were real but they were also theatrical. Her gasps belonged to someone else.

Beth loomed in the doorway. "Are you for real?"

Molly nodded into the quilt. She shook her head. She wanted to stop crying, but holding it in made the sobs bounce out erratically.

"Relax," Beth said. "They're not that innocent."

"But your job," Molly said. "And the dog."

Beth paused, perhaps thinking of what James had said, wondering who the murderer was. There were only so many possibilities. Maybe, hopefully, Beth thought something worse had happened. But nothing was worse, not for Beth.

"Where's Chowder?" Beth said.

It wasn't fair to tell her this way, earning her pity first. Even though Molly didn't like the dog taking up half the bed or his white hair on her black wardrobe or his steaming shit, the thin skin of plastic bag over her hand her only protection, or, most of all, how Beth hugged and fondled him instead of hugging and fondling Molly, now Beth was alone—stuck in Hurlbut with all these kids and no Chowder. What if Beth ended up not really gay, or what if the relationship grew too serious for Molly and she left? Or, most likely, what if Beth dumped her right now?

"He's dead," Molly said. She'd blown her load earlier, describing the incident to James with nuance and remorse. Now the plain truth was out, ugly and unwieldy. She sponged her tears with the corner of her flannel. Then she described what had happened.

Beth shook her head. She set her fingers on her temple and closed her eyes. When Molly was done, they went minutes without speaking, Beth raising a finger whenever Molly opened her mouth. After ages, Beth said, "Show me."

"What do you mean?" Molly shuddered, flashing on Beth pulling the soggy corpse from the Charles.

Beth put on her boots, and Molly had no choice but to do so too. After the room of cake smoke, Prospect Street was like the top of a mountain, the atmosphere so thin you had to breathe fast to get enough. They took Bow Street to Memorial Drive and crossed to the river.

There were a couple pinpricks of light in the sky, probably airplanes and satellites but maybe planets. The ice on the river was lit white as though illuminated from below. Beth lowered her foot to the ice but Molly stopped her. "It's dangerous."

That was all Beth needed to hear, logical Beth. When her cheeks caught the glow of the river, they were wet. Molly reached out to hold her, but Beth shoved her away, lip tangled under her teeth, eyes hooded and fierce.

They watched the river for ages. Molly switched from one foot to the other in the damp cold. She was dying to know if Beth would dump her. She wasn't ready to give up their time: going to old movies on big screens, traveling to the city to taste new teas, walking with Beth by the Charles and discussing the uncanny valley or gender performance in Dante, Molly hustling to keep up, trying to be funny at least, if not smart. So it was a boring life, who cared? No one was wild forever. Would she really rather snort lactose in the bathroom of a naked party in Jamaica Plain?

The hole was a dim patch now on the ice. A shell must have frozen over since that afternoon, capping Chowder with a roof, a warped view of the winter sky.

Beth walked back to Hurlbut. The tendons in Molly's neck tightened, watching her go. She could follow or take the foot-bridge to Allston. But the cake, and the mess in the suite. At least she should clean up. Then, if Beth wanted, she'd leave.

Beth prepared for bed as though Molly weren't there. Molly's hands shook as she pushed the deteriorating sponge over the burners. She was about to wash the cake out of the pan when she discovered the inside was fluffy and wet with blue explosions where the berries had broken under heat. The high temperature had flash-cooked the interior into a silky loaf. Molly dug cake out of the black pocket and heaped it on a plate. The cake looked like rice or porridge but tasted of delicate fruity clouds. She was hungry enough to scarf it all. But instead, she carried it in to Beth.

"What's this?" Beth asked when Molly offered the plate from across the room.

"Blueberry vanilla hot chocolate cake." That sounded better than it was.

Beth took a bite. She made a face but kept eating. She hated sweets, but maybe this was a grudging sign of forgiveness. Or, at least, Beth was delaying kicking her out.

Beth turned off the light. Molly stood there in the dark. Then, because she hadn't been told not to, she undressed. She laid herself down stiffly on the bed, facing the ceiling, as far from Beth as possible.

"I know he's just a dog," Beth said, voice shaky, breath sour with stress and travel.

Chowder had been her main concern for years, her prodigy, her heir. Beth was talking crap. But Molly didn't know what to say either. At all. "He did his job," she finally mumbled. "And now he's gone." James's words sounded lame in her throat.

"You shouldn't have let him off the leash." Beth shifted onto her back, a quarter roll toward Molly. "Now I'll have to pay off James Masterson. Jesus."

"I'm sorry." Molly could go on apologizing forever, shaving chips off the block of what she'd done. She reached through the sheets and found Beth's wrist. She squeezed it, like she used to do in Girl Scouts, in a circle while singing. The gesture was stupid, but it was all she managed. Beth turned in the blue light and studied Molly like she was from a different world.

"I fucked up. But I have to tell you something."

"What?" Beth sounded skeptical, like Molly had killed another animal or corrupted poor James Masterson in yet more twisted ways.

Molly took a breath. "I'm in love with you." The words came out like bad acting. She wanted to swallow them immediately, delete them from the air.

Beth studied Molly's face. "That's crazy. That's rat-shit crazy."

Beth would yell at Molly all through the next morning. She would cry every night before bed for weeks, sleep with the leash wrapping her forearm like tefillin. The leather would go soft from how hard she wound it. She wouldn't say she loved Molly back for months. Some days she'd barely even look at her. Molly would suffer. Maybe more than she deserved.

But for now, Molly and Beth stared together at the same ceiling, frosted with moonlit curves, the cake a grounding weight in their bellies. Molly matched her breath to Beth's and focused on the love gelling between them, however hard it was, sometimes, to find.

Sunny Talks

HUNCHED OVER MY COMPUTER IN MY CUBICLE, I prepare for my nephew's visit by watching one of his YouTube videos. His backdrop is his bedroom, the walls painted black, centaur and mermaid posters freshly hung. His mascots, he calls them. He pops into the frame, flaunting his naked, scar-free chest. He's fifteen but looks ten. His wrists are so frail, his shoulders so narrow, that I worry that he'll break his arms with his eager, sweeping gestures. His audience is ten or twenty thousand people who litter his page with rainbow emojis, kissing emojis, shining sun emojis, interrupted by trolls reminding him he's a damaged and mutilated female.

"Welcome to Sunny's channel." He rolls his eyes like everyone knows already. Sunny was always his name, so when people threaten to publish his real name he has a laugh, thrusting his head back against the wall of his bedroom, which is beside my older sister's bedroom in their little house in Shrewsbury, though Sunny doesn't reveal where he dispatches from; he's learned from millennial elders on the platform at least the basics of safe internet practices.

He lifts the rabbit my sister bought him and holds it to the camera, pink pads swelling to blot out the screen. The rabbit died a few months after this video, of nose cancer.

"My assistant," Sunny says. "Almond Senior." He bounces the rabbit's haunches. "Pronouns: they/them." He snorts. "Almond Senior's nonbinary." The rabbit's cute, cancer-filled nose presses against Sunny's cute, little boy nose. "So trendy, now, aren't you?"

I pull back from the screen into the green light of the office. I've watched the video a dozen times, awaiting this moment, my breath so quick it's audible, perking my ears for Sunny's tone. Is the joke that the rabbit has an identity, or is the joke that the identity is nonbinary?

Sunny crops the frame at his waist, as though he has hips to hide. He updates his perspective regularly, on crucial queer Gen Z issues such as pansexuality, passing privilege, cisnormativity, he/him lesbians, PGPs, chasers, and demi-romanticism. He applies gel to his hair so it crests sweetly over his forehead, a neighbor boy from a fifties sitcom.

I live hundreds of miles from Sunny now, but this evening my sister will drop him at my apartment in Trenton. Tomorrow Sunny and I will attend a convention of trans YouTubers in Philadelphia. Sunny invited me a few weeks back, explaining that it wasn't cool to go with his mom, that he preferred me, his aunt, which was fishy, because he loves my sister, but I guess everyone grows up sometime. Last week, he sent a video message of himself singing "Streets of Philadelphia" with a plastic bell (the crack drawn in Sharpie) nested in his soft disc of hair and a portrait of Ben Franklin taped to the wall behind.

I pat my blouse to absorb the sweat from my palms. Tonight I'll discuss my identity with Sunny, tell him what's been true my whole life, though only now is there language for it. I hate to burden a kid with my issues, but he's the only trans person I know.

"Uh, the write-up?" Eric says, looming over my desk. My colleagues don't look directly at me, as though I could infect them through the eyes. But I hold out hope that Eric could become a friend. He visits my desk instead of emailing me. His earring is either queer or cheesy, same with his spiked, thinning hair. Once I'm more comfortable in my body I'll ask him for a drink at the sports bar.

I pinch the report from my printer tray and clap it into a folder. Eric snatches the file as though I'll change my mind.

That evening my sister Jen arrives on my doorstep, chest out, proud. She's done everything for Sunny at every stage, each intervention and treatment on schedule. She even pulled him from Shrewsbury High because of bullying, though she's unqualified to homeschool. I'm shocked by how she's handled his transition, with good cheer and hearty forward momentum. When I was thirteen, bow-legged with a rag of hair, the only person in our family with a Boston accent, Jen convinced her classmates that I was an unsavory male cousin. I still brace for her to call me Leon Jenkins.

Jen pats my shoulder. Her ponytail swings. "Thanks for taking him."

"Who is it this time?" I whisper.

Confusion flares across her face, quickly snuffed. There isn't any tryst. Of course not. She's checking into some motel to await her precious son. Jen thumps into my apartment, avoiding the question as she heads down the hall to the bathroom. Sunny flings his duffle onto the stoop and embraces me. He's the only person who's never noticed the failure of my hugs, so he's the only person I enjoy hugging. I'm forty-seven, frumpy, misunderstood by all as asexual, but still, I'm his cool aunt.

"You've grown up so much," I say.

He runs a palm through his hair. Such a boy gesture. Where did he learn it?

I set out a bowl filled with puffy bears coated in cheese powder, Sunny's favorite snack, a rare find among the bleak offerings of Trenton grocery stores. Sunny curls on the couch and helps himself.

Jen finishes her water and refills the glass. She pats her thighs, securely pressed into yoga pants. "I'm leaving."

I haven't seen Jen without my parents in years. If I keep her an hour, we could get to Eric. We could analyze my crush the way we used to with hers as children, scheming into the night. "I thought we could chat a little."

Jen scrapes a finger over her phone as though she could

draw up a message. "Well. I guess we should talk over Sunny's stuff, anyway."

"I'm not a child," he says, mouth packed with cheese.

"You're fifteen," Jen says. "Don't push this, kiddo." She hooks him into her arms and squeezes his skinny shoulders. His hair licks up against her sweater. The apartment is so full of life I could dance.

Instead, I follow Jen to the door, dragging my shirt down over my hips, scouring my brain for a clever opening to detain her. How relaxing it would be to slump against her large frame in front of the TV, even just for an hour. At the threshold she launches into Sunny's needs: he won't eat chickpeas or meat or radishes or red jelly; he has lotion in his bag for the dry patch on his elbow. She packed a workbook in case he can fit in a little studying. "He gets overstimulated. He'll want to stay the whole day tomorrow, but maybe skip the last bit."

I take notes, though I know everything already.

"Remember when we went up Monadnock, when he was six?" she asks. Jen carried Sunny halfway up the mountain, his body flipped over her shoulder, pigtails dangling.

"You worry about him too much." My words are sharper than I intend.

"He's a kid."

Besides his fifth-grade trip to Manhattan—the last school year Sunny attended as a girl—he's never left New England. "He's a teenager. He'll be fine."

"Don't make me regret this."

"Hey," I say, softening, playing along with her story.

"Ditch your friend. We'll watch movies or something. Come on, Jen. It'll be nice." Somewhere toward midnight, Sunny asleep between us, our bodies washed in the aqua light of the TV, Jen will apologize for how she treated me when we were kids. I'll laugh and say it's nothing. And it will be nothing, somehow, suddenly. A glow will ignite between us, and our relationship will revert to how it was before I hit puberty. We'll hug a normal hug. And ever after: weekly calls like regular siblings. Conversations that aren't about Sunny.

She waves me away. As she ducks into the car, her face strains.

I sit with Sunny, him on the couch, me on the desk chair. He clutches his phone, skinny limbs tangled. I have to pee, but if I leave even for a second, he'll drift away on the currents of the internet. What can I ask next? How's puberty? Have you discovered what romance is yet? What are my sister's secrets? Sunny and I like each other—he's my only nibling, a term he taught me—but we've only spent time together with family. We've diced tubers for holiday meals and raised our voices to compete with conversations about baseball and acid reflux. We've never talked about anything serious.

"So," I say. "How's math class? You must have math class, right?" I want to slap myself.

His knee bounces. "Not class, really. I have, like, workbooks."

I arrange the cheese bears on the coffee table. "What about language arts?"

"I have a workbook for that too. The cover has, like, tumbling letters to symbolize the vast and dynamic field of English-language literature."

"Science?"

"Workbook." He seizes a fistful of bears.

"Health?" One regret is that I can't fully see Sunny as a boy. He's used male pronouns since age eleven and never developed female sex characteristics, but, although he looks like a boy and is shaped like a boy and I've never botched his pronouns, I trust him more than I'd trust any boy. I give him more credit. And I like him more, which is a betrayal.

He raises and lowers his palms like a scale. "Workbook."

"Sunny." I roll back on my chair—the floor is so sloped that every minute we're farther apart. I resolve not to pee until I tell him who I am. I realize I've been mutilating a cheese bear only when it explodes on my knee. I ball the bear's remains into a marble and flick it away. "I've been thinking about stuff. About me."

He blinks. His big eyes, his towhead, his jittering leg, glancing down at his phone every second. Jen's right. He's a child. I shouldn't dump my sour adult laundry all over him. "Never mind."

His attention snaps back to the screen. "So, I just found out? There's gonna be these guys at the conference tomorrow. Emmerson and Henry?" His thumbs are all over the screen, satisfying bleeps pulsing up. "These transmed assholes.

They're always mocking kids in their comments. We have to go to their panel, okay?"

"Okay." My legs twitch. "I guess I'll retire, then."

Sunny looks up, surprised. The sky still has light. "That's all right, Lillia." The baby-talk way he still says my name gives me chills. His features crunch together. His fans call this his old man face, which he makes when discussing the grimmest community comments: *My grandpa's dying but I'm not ready for him to see how I look now. My mom took my period stuff so I'd have to ask for it back. My parents call me "it" and the dog's name.*

Once in my room, I'm trapped. It's only eight, and the bathroom is off the living room. I'm in my nightgown already and I don't want to pass Sunny so exposed. My breasts are loose, hot and itchy, too heavy, showing through the cotton. And I'm too overwhelmed to talk to him anymore, afraid I'll blurt my secret. Through the closed door, Sunny calls Jen, complaining that his friends at the conference have already gathered. "Yes, Mom, friends from the internet," he says. "They count as friends."

I seize the doorknob. I'll drive him to Philly, wait in the car with a book while he socializes. But I can't lurk in proximity to such cool, self-actualized young people. I'll kill myself. I'm glad Sunny got hormone blockers, of course I am. I'm proud of my sister for realizing what was going on, for getting him to a specialist before puberty started, for not giving in to the anti-trans panic that's hyped up even more since the election. The technology was new even to me. But sometimes I can't bear the fact that, if I were born a bit later, all I would've needed was injections. That my body never had to bloom into these curves.

I sometimes half-wake in a panic, convinced I've just turned thirteen, that my breasts have pushed against the skin, that I'm one day late for intervention. That now I'll be stuck in this body forever, terrified of sex because my shape could never bump up against someone else, so my crushes burn out like stars. When I blink awake and I'm forty-seven, the option for blockers having passed thirty-four years ago, it's not comforting.

Would Sunny have snorted if I'd told him I want to live between the genders? Would he have said, "So trendy"? If I'm not going all the way, he might think I'm not serious. And I don't want a beard. I don't want a bald spot. I fear what anger T could draw out. I sink under my sheets, braiding my legs so I don't wet the bed.

The conference is far enough outside the city that there aren't even sidewalks. We enter the massive bubble of a building under a double banner of the generic queer rainbow and the specialized trans rainbow. Doors all around the giant mushroom atrium discharge hip youngsters. Girls who still read as boys with hair swished into elegant up-dos, colt-like in their heels, boys who still read as girls with mop heads and high athletic socks.

There are kids here who even I, with my YouTube research, cannot identify as trans, trotting so easily in their gender it's like they never had to win it. There are kids aiming for and achieving a space so exactly in the middle that you couldn't guess what color birth blanket the doctor once wrapped them in: baby faces with voices that dustings of T or hours of training have frozen into a curious, second-look register too low for a girl, too high for a guy. Their hair sculpted into short shapes stuck between butch and fey, their bodies either skinny or overweight, because it's the weights between, I've learned, like my own, that telegraph gender most clearly.

At registration, Sunny paws through a spread of name-tags. If only my name were less feminine and I had a channel listed like everyone else. I once came out in a DM to a trans YouTuber whose profile made him look older than he probably was. His answer was so spammy and generic—*Go for it! Age matters not!*—that I never reached out again.

My conference registration was a hundred dollars. I'm still in the red from my move, and every month I go deeper, eating plain pasta to add to my surgery fund. Sunny doesn't know the cost of the conference and so snatches the gift tote with a victory shout, counting the free pin, free condom, free hamburger-shaped eraser, and free pack of nuts as an unimaginable windfall.

Off the atrium shoots a hall lined with doors. Each door

boasts a sandwich board with the day's panel schedule, a fresh lineup every hour. At the end of the hall is the auditorium for celebrity events and the keynote. Nut packets and half-sucked lozenges litter the floor.

Participants study me, as though decoding this middle-aged woman's purpose. Am I Sunny's mother? No; Jen's cameo is Sunny's most popular video—her smug appearance as perfect mom—*you gotta do right by your kid*—so if they know him, they know Jen. I should've brought a hoodie, but when I dress masculine everyone thinks I'm a lesbian. I've dated few men, but in my butch periods I haven't landed any. Until I can hover deep enough in the middle to range beyond lesbian—with a micro-dose of T hardening my face and speckling my chin with hair—until I can look more like a girly boy instead of a boyish girl, until I can scrape these breasts off my ribs and stand up straight, what I wear seems secondary. Except for here.

I dodge through the crowd. I've stepped inside my computer, everyone newly dimensional and visible, for once, from head to toe. There's Irish Danny Ray Kyle, a tiny copy of Justin Bieber, trailed by waifs in pancake makeup. There's Paulie G from Norway, who, at twenty, is a community elder. Paulie G transitioned late—"late" is seventeen—so his hips are wide, a detail he's disguised in his videos. My heart pulls for him as he shuffles by.

A pair of famous transgirl sisters strolls past. The older one transitioned second, after a suicide attempt, coming out on the younger one's channel with her wrists wrapped and her voice too soft for the mic. The sisters' red hair is tied into contrasting scrunchies, and they skip through the conference collecting greetings like they were never sad a day in their lives. Maybe transitioning is like that. Once you settle into your new form, a peace descends and, for the first time in years, you skip.

Kids clamp Sunny in hugs. "Sunny Talks," "My internet crush," "You're so mini in real life." He lets them linger in his arms. Sunny's wonderful with the weak. That must've been why I thought I could talk to him.

"Emmerson's panel is next," he says. "I'm going to ask a question. Like, a super pointed question."

I'm about to ask what the big deal is about a question, but he's not in school, hasn't been for two years.

"No one challenges that kid. Like, ever."

As we pick our way up the hall, Sunny spots a friend loitering by the water fountain, hands in pockets, chin high, a little older, around nineteen. Shiny of face and puffy of body, the friend sits between genders. Whenever I encounter someone in between, their success or failure predicts my future attempt. If they're attractive, if they achieve the middle, my heart soars for my own transition. If they're unappealing or settle too clearly in the camp of man or woman, I despair. This person is tall and soft with a haircut that starts short on the brow, piles up all swishy at the crest of the head, and shortens severely against the neck. They've achieved the middle, but they aren't attractive.

Sunny says, "Button's channel dominates," then hugs them in his easy, happy way, like a kid who spent his life ricocheting between siblings. He introduces me as his favorite aunt, and Button bobs on their heels.

"Sunny's family!" they cry. "You need a hug."

"That's okay."

Button leans in. My elbows jut out and I clap their shoulders, hunching my back to keep space. I hide my face against their chest. And then I'm sheltered in the hug. In the dark heat of Button's sweatshirt, I will never have to make decisions. My arms soften, like they never do, and, for once, a hug feels nice.

"Wow," Button says, face twisted in confusion. "Are you mad at me?" I step back.

"She hugs strange," says Sunny. "But she's a cool person."

Heaviness drops through me. I study the corporate pattern woven into the carpet.

Button turns to Sunny. "I upset the lady. Yo, hey. Don't freak. At the beginning of my transition I was a rough hugger too."

I freeze. But of course Button knows. Why else am I here? Relief blows through me in a cold wind.

"Don't despair, beautiful." Button claps my shoulder. "It takes time to get used to a new body. And you totally mostly pass as a chick."

"Oh," I say, cheeks tingling. They have me the wrong way round, but it's something. A panel releases. Conference-goers push and shove, a bright, heady jostle. Button's big face bobs over the shoulders of teens.

"No, dude." Sunny's voice strains. "Hold up, no. She's not trans."

Button's lip twitches. They bow. "Ah. Apologies."

Sunny grabs my hand and beelines through the crowd. We squeeze past clumps of kids on either side. "I'm sorry, Lillia. That was not okay. That was so not okay." He breathes unevenly, like he used to at the beginning of panic attacks. "You totally don't look trans. Like, at all."

"It's okay," I say. "It's not an insult." I'm about to say Button was right, is the thing, when Sunny stops and stares at me, cheeks glossy.

"You're right," he says. "I can't believe I never thought of that. Of course it's not." He wipes his wrist across his forehead. "What's wrong with me?"

We take our seats for the panel. Sunny rocks in the chair beside mine, rubbing his knees, intent on the dais, on which sit three panelists. Two are cis-passing boys in their late teens. They could be brothers, but one has an English accent, the other a tweed blazer. These are Henry and Emmerson, according to the table tents—Sunny says transguys all have names like Victorian heirs. Both have thick arms crossed, freckles that rise into zits over the top of their noses, and crew cuts.

The other panelist, Wellcamp, possibly a college student, leans toward boy, though I'm not supposed to guess like that. They have a strong jaw, deep-set eyes, a blue bob, and silver nail polish.

"The dude with the blazer is Emmerson. He's such a dick," Sunny says, with reverence. "Him and the other guy hate Wellcamp. They made, like, this stupid 'exposed' video about how Wellcamp's a transtrender."

Sunny hasn't shared an opinion on transtrenders, but he has a certain smugness about having started early. He posts shirtless childhood photos, with hidden ponytails and thick bangs. Commenters cast doubt that he was assigned female at birth. Really, the signs were subtler than that. As a child, Sunny wasn't a boy to me, per se, though not exactly a girl either. He was a wild, genderless thing: charming and silly and free, forever hyper or bereft. More weasel than kid. And I watched him closely, knowing I'd never have my own child, since pregnancy would swell my body further in the wrong direction.

A lady introduces the panelists. She's from the national gender outreach hotline that sponsored the conference. She explains that the participants will "debate the core of trans identity, along with issues of permission and fundamental definition." She retires to the front row, stooped and mousy, glancing around like she fears attack.

"So," says Emmerson, thumping his arms down on the table. "I guess it's time to sniff out the 'core of trans identity.'"

"Nasty, mate," says Henry, and they both giggle.

"I brought some notes," says Wellcamp, tapping a battered composition book, as though the relevant information will agitate to the surface. "We could open with the theoretical and home in on IRL?"

Emmerson checks the door. "You know what, screw this." He aims his nose at Wellcamp. "Everyone knows why they put us together. Let's talk about why you pose as trans to get more followers and, like, minority cred."

"She doesn't even have gender dysphoria," Henry says. "Ask her, mate."

At the pronoun, air sucks out of the audience. I cross my arms over my chest. At home, I have a set of expensive binders, still stored in their wrappers. When I try them on they hurt as badly as the kids say and worse, due to my soft, aging torso.

Wellcamp leans back, shaking blue hair off their face. The way their hair moves—of a piece and so dry—it's obvious it's a wig. "I don't believe in gender dysphoria."

Emmerson and Henry groan.

Wellcamp closes their eyes. "Can't we rethink our language? Why is our community so negative? What about gender euphoria for once?"

Surely there are moments, many moments, in a transition that trigger euphoria. Like when I ordered the binders, or when I pin my hair back so fiercely it looks short. I turn to Sunny for approval, but his mouth is tight.

Henry's skin brightens under his freckles: "Of course it's negative to be trans. You're born wrong, so what the fuck, of course! You want what you'll never have. I'll never have a normal willy. I'll never have inbred male confidence. I'll never get those extra little pushes forward a real boy gets one billion times before he even knows what gender is."

"All I'm saying," says Wellcamp, "is that isn't everyone's way. Some people make changes out of joy." They spin a hand over their front, their sparkly top ruffling. "I got top surgery out of joy." They point out a patch on their wrist like an acid burn. "I got phalloplasty out of joy." They dangle their fingers over the rim of the table. "I'm wearing nail polish and this hair because it all makes me happy."

"Then why?" Emmerson's voice is so strained he's barely audible. "What motivates you if you were so happy before? Why pay a hundred thousand dollars to slice up your junk if you're literally spinning around a mountaintop singing about joy?"

Sunny's hands clench his chair. Does he remember my sister's fights with his father, a stumpy architect who left when Sunny was three? Last year Sunny wrote him a letter. His father responded: *I don't have a son.* If Nathan had stayed, Sunny would be halfway through the wrong puberty, miserable and silent. Bangs in his eyes, shoulders hunched around breasts, thinner even than he is now, his voice low and dead. Me at his age.

"She's fucked, dude," says Emmerson to Henry. He turns to Wellcamp. "You're discrediting our community."

"Why do you even care?" Sunny's voice breaks the arguing, and the panelists turn. He stands on his chair, slim and tufted as a dandelion, swaying high. I raise my arms instinctively, ready to catch him if he falls.

"Sunny Talks?" Emmerson's voice softens. "Dude, what's up."

"Wellcamp's fine." Sunny's voice rings through the canned air. "They're, like, probably a fine person." A shaky sigh heaves out of him. "So leave them alone."

Wellcamp is as abashed as Emmerson and Henry, all three slouching like children caught squabbling, which, really, they are. Sunny lingers on the chair, applause sinking into his skinny shoulders, rotating his golden face for the crowd.

For lunch, I drive Sunny to a cheesesteak joint whose vegetarian option, according to online photos, is crushed tofu coated with a plastic skin of cheese. I pledge to order it in solidarity. "I'm so proud of you," I say, bouncing in the squeaky booth. "You really told him."

"I know," he says, his voice tiny, thrilled.

Heat prickles the back of my neck. Sunny spoke up for the nonbinaries. Maybe I can talk to him after all, in the privacy of the car, driving to the afternoon panels.

Sunny smooths a crease in the laminated menu. "I really thought I'd chicken out. Like, I didn't even know I was doing it until I was up there, like, doing it."

The waitress sets sweating glasses of water between us. "Ladies? What can I get you?"

I don't register her words until I've placed our orders, and I turn back to Sunny. The vinyl cushion has depressed behind his head, as though he's forced his spine against it hard enough to swallow him.

"Oh, Sunny," I say. "It was an honest mistake."

He hardens his jaw. His focus slides off me. He's acting like he did as a little girl, going limp at any slight. "I don't know what you're talking about." He rises against the booth, shoulders squared. We chew our crumpled soy in silence.

After lunch we attend two more panels, one on T distribution and then a reading of self-published memoir excerpts from teens who, a year or two out from their transitions, are eager to reflect. "Life was hard," reads one kid. "I concerned my mom by declining PB and J."

"Sunny," I say, en route to the keynote. "I'm sorry about lunch. Look." My voice wobbles. "I sorta get how it feels."

"Don't," he says, through teeth, his shoulders up, like an animal under threat.

"Okay. Okay." My face relaxes into flabby indifference. The day has lost its point. I want it over, want to be alone in my bed, darkness falling out the window until I give up and turn on the light. "Maybe we should head out? Jen said you might get tired."

"I'm not a baby."

"She treats you that way, doesn't she? Sometimes?"

His eyes narrow. "Why do you care? You're always so weird about her."

Kids pass in waves, cramping me in. "I don't know." A child jostles me. "I guess I'm jealous, kind of."

"That makes zero sense."

He's genuinely confused. He trots to the auditorium, knees high, like a child.

The whole conference is in attendance. We pass a

transboy with a dark wedge of hair, a minor TikTok heart-throb. In person, he's so shockingly young that it's upsetting to see him move through the world unattached to a parent.

I should be grateful that the world changed in time for Sunny. If I were his mother, my feeling would be pure. But as it is, I wish the shift hadn't happened too late for me to ever be beautiful in my right body but too soon for me to die in the peace of never having known another way.

I haven't checked the subject of the keynote, because we should be on the highway by now. The administrator introduces someone named Minsie Slater, who will share their life story. The speaker ascends the stage and leans their elbows on the lectern. They clear their throat and describe themself as a real estate agent and homeowner. Minsie is older than me, with a dense lick of silver hair, a single long earring like a twisting bar of light, and curiously pink skin. They have thin, wise eyes. Big hands cradle the printout of their speech. I can't determine their original gender assignment, but I don't want to. The room goes silent, agitated. There's a quality to the way they spread their elbows on the podium, the softness of their face against its serious set, that makes you want to perk up and be good.

Minsie peers around the hall. When they open their mouth they speak like they're sitting next to everyone, individually, in some quiet room: "One evening, early in puberty, I took a bath." They push their glasses up higher on their face. "I laid washcloths on parts of my body that I preferred not to visit. As the cloth dried, it shrank and suctioned to my skin like plaster casts. Only then could I look at myself, at this body with each bad patch redacted. The door was closed. I'm telling you this because that evening in Rapid City, decades before you were born, was the one time I felt okay."

In the gelled quiet of the auditorium, I sink into the water of my own long-ago bath. Jen was beside me, though we were big enough that our elbows and knees bumped. Our mother must've been in a hurry. Dressed for a restaurant, shining us up for some babysitter. In the jostle of wet limbs and the metallic tang of the water, I gave myself over to her scrubbing, disappearing my body, until her sponge caught my nipple and I howled. Jen gaped as my scream sliced the air and left it in scraps around us.

"Are you okay?" my mother asked, certain I was. She knew the borders of my body. She knew better than I did what hurt.

My nipples ached. Soon they'd swell like Jen's, but I could never stick my chest out like her, calling them bomb-bombs and rattling them at neighbors. And the way Jen watched, tense arm gripping the rim of the tub, made me shrink back in the cooling water. "I'm okay," I said, too many times. Jen's face sagged. She mumbled, "Why's she gotta be so weird?"

Minsie bows over their printed speech. The chatter in the audience rises. "I have my notes here." They lift the page. Stage lights shine through a block of text. "It's all about my private body feelings. My relationships. Coming out. My 'journey.' But you know what?" Minsie plucks their glasses off their face, fingers trembling. Maybe they're older than they look. "Fuck all that. I don't have to tell any of you shit. None of us do."

A pocket of quiet opens across the room, like when a musician finishes a song, and the audience decides together not to bust the mood. The blank air swells inside me. I have to transition. I've always planned to, really. Whether it will take months or decades, I've known I'd come to this. And with Minsie up there, statuesque with their soft skin and square head, I've never considered my position has any advantage, that I could ever be all right, much less great, powerful, flinging aside my notes before two hundred beautiful teens.

The silence bursts and the crowd roars, and it's like they're roaring for my choice. Girls with bony knees and big noses bash their hands together; boys with styled hair and evergreen hoodies throw their fists. They leap up and wave. "Don't tell us shit," chants a kid next to us. This from kids who've spent their lives documenting their stories, who've offered the world every grain of their shit.

Sunny claps halfheartedly, glancing over his shoulder. "I gotta talk to Emmerson. I don't like how we left it."

"Shouldn't we start home?" Cheers ring out around us.

"But when will I ever be in a place like this again?"

He's right. When will *I* ever be in a place like this? Many fewer times than him. Together, we cut through the mass of attendees, shoulders brushing as participants push past. Among the sea of children, older people have materialized. A guy my age takes a selfie with two women only a little younger. A man leans on a walker by a modular wall. A couple in their sixties shares chicken tenders from a napkin. I set my shoulders back and stride ahead.

The afterparty is in the parking lot, stuck in a fog of chill. Tiki torches flicker, so many tiki torches that the pavement is clinically bright. A table offers troughs of potato chips and candy. Dimpled two-liter bottles of Coke.

We find Emmerson, presiding over a knot of younger transguys. His face makes the shapes of grievance as the little boys study his every twitch.

"Come with me," Sunny says. "Please? I need to talk to him."

Emmerson spots us and turns quickly away. I should warn Sunny to proceed with caution, but I don't want to get caught up in their spat. Let him figure it out. "You go."

His face breaks, half hurt, half confused. "Ugh, fine." He heads on without me.

Finally, blood shivers through my limbs. I can walk anywhere. I can talk to anyone. The freedom is itchy, bloating my chest, too airy to suffer. I scan the crowd. Even a hello will be some shuffle forward. I slow as I pass a woman with a satisfying rope of a braid and the same wide shoulders as Jen. Jen, tall and curvy, bigger than all her boyfriends, twice the size of Sunny's father: I wish, for the first time all day, that she were here. But Minsie steps out in front of me. "No alcohol in child land," they say, wagging a tiny cup.

Up close, they're so much smaller, compact and dense. "Right," I say, though I haven't checked.

Minsie peers into their drink. "They could at least provide normal cups. So we could pound the juice."

"That's how they stay slim." Boys skip past, hair flopping.

"Are you a speaker?"

"I'm here with my nephew." If only Sunny were beside me, charming Minsie with his boundless energy.

"Two trans in one family. That's rare."

"Yeah." My breath catches. "Actually, though, I wasn't born a guy." My knees loosen. I fear Minsie will think me a poseur, but why does it matter? I'll never meet them again. For practice, I say it, finally: "I'm nonbinary." The words sound trendy, hopeful, like a geezer in a novelty T-shirt.

Minsie's face remains bland. "Are you having a good conference?"

"I guess." Did I really just tell them? Was it so easy and stupid? I don't even know if I'm having a good conference. I take a breath. "But thank you. For asking." I pinch my elbow until it stings. "What you said about the bath. Your old, like, bath? That sort of got me."

Minsie looks beyond me, my cheesy words hanging. Kids tangle together in parking spots, staring at one another like they can't believe the night is real, too stupefied to even touch. "I think you're the only one who listened." They snort. Their nose is broad and flexible, sturdy, like a bull's. "I wasn't trying to be a rock star. I don't know why I didn't think about it before. But I was up there, jabbering, and suddenly it was like clouds parting or whatever shit. Of course these kids have moved on from any stupid freak out. And here's this fossil, spewing."

"Yes," I say, too loudly. "It's galling."

Minsie's focus wanders down to find me. They offer a parsimonious nod. "You want a drink? A real one?" They say it like I asked, like I begged, like they're grudgingly consenting.

"I can't tonight."

"Well." Minsie's cheeks brighten, like a candle lit up inside their head. "Tonight isn't the last night on earth."

"No," I whisper. Are they hitting on me? Their breath burns my forehead. They step closer. Those handsome, slender eyes, vibrant slivers in skin that's invitingly soft, mature. How lovely, a night full of Minsie's attention.

Sunny appears at my side, face strained, dancing on his toes. "Can we go?"

My first instinct is to agree, yes, of course, whatever he wants. But I'm trying to give myself time here. I make myself pause, say, "I'm having a conversation."

Sunny groans. "But you said you wanted to go home, and, like, if we have to go home now, that's chill." He peers at the bank of cars, ours somewhere out there, like he could will me toward it. He's had an intense day. Meeting friends who only ever lived in the flat circles of their avatars, finding them thrilling or disappointing or overwhelming or irritating. Speaking before an audience. Being among other kids, en masse, for the first time in years.

My mouth twitches, still stuck in the shape of gratitude for Minsie's invitation. "We can go soon, Sunny. Can you give me a minute?"

"We could have cheese bears and hang out?"

The plan sounds so sweet, so cozy, that half of me melts toward it.

"Yes, dear," says Minsie, their voice pitching high, as though Sunny were years younger. "Me and your—what term do you prefer? There isn't a neutral for aunt and uncle, as far as I'm aware—are talking."

"Wait, what?" Sunny stares between me and Minsie. He takes in my whole body, top to bottom. His eyes are shiny, extra bright, absorbing. "Lillia? What do they they mean?"

We stare at one another, arms loose, at a loss. The crowds around us have shifted, so we're washed up on our own lonely ring of concrete. "It's okay," I say. "Hey. Sunny. Can we talk about this later? I was just telling Minsie. Like, about me."

His mouth knots into a red ball. "I mean, Mom said you were like that when you were little. That's why she told me to invite you. She said I should talk to you about it or whatever." He rolls his eyes to the dark sky. "I thought she was being annoying. I thought she meant just, like, a thousand years ago. Like you were a tomboy or something dumb."

Sunny's words needle my skin. He and Jen have discussed me like I'm his age. Anger should follow, or humiliation. How can he stand there, dismissing the struggle of my life? I want to snap at him, send him away. But I swallow. I force myself to think. Because maybe Jen was trying. But maybe Jen was trying. Maybe she threw herself into helping Sunny because she couldn't go back and help me when we were kids.

"It's a lot more than that," I say. "It always has been." I take a breath. "I'm good at hiding."

"No." Sunny's face screws up like I've told him he was

adopted, like everything he thought he knew is a lie. "I would've noticed."

"Adults have inner lives too, you know," Minsie says. "It would be good of the youth to remember."

"Shut up, okay?" says Sunny. "Seriously, who even are you? You're just, like, some random stranger."

"They're the speaker," I say, willing the bratty edge to soften from his voice. "Come on, Sunny. Be polite."

"But you're lying, right?" he says. "You're trying to fit in or something."

I search for words to make him feel better. "Don't worry," I say. "Nothing has to change."

"Of course it does." Minsie's face hardens into a mask of patience. "Son, you're being trusted with information here. What are you going to do with it?"

"But she lied to me," he squeaks. "She had the same shit, all this time, and she didn't even try to help? You're telling me that's cool?"

"I'm sorry," I say. But I couldn't have helped him. I was lost in my own swamp.

"You don't know what it was like for me."

"I was there."

He steps toward me, humiliation wet in his eyes. "Shut up. Just shut up."

"Come on now, kid," Minsie says. "Have a little empathy."

"Get out of here," Sunny says. "Why are you even still here? I'm trying to talk to my aunt."

At *aunt*, Minsie's finger shoots toward Sunny's face. "Cut it out right now. I know you're surprised. But take a breath. You need to put your shit aside and support your family member."

Sunny shrinks, hands rising in protection. He tracks the finger like it will stab his eye. I grab his shoulders and pull him to me. His frame is frail against my stomach. He shivers like he might cry.

"Leave him alone," I spit. "He's a child."

Minsie steps back, guilty finger limp, like a snapped twig. My adrenaline—still shooting through me in circles—feels silly. "I'm sorry," Minsie says. "I hated him calling you that."

And Minsie is right: it felt wrong, suddenly wrong, to be "aunt" again. But that's good, that's exciting. Everything changing so quickly. "Just leave." My voice cracks. Sunny burrows into me. Minsie squints, a jewel of moisture caught in their eye, then turns to slink off between tiki torches. As they push farther away, past teenagers and stands of soda, their heavy hips upsetting a bowl of pretzels, I remember their invitation, and panic flutters into my throat—I didn't get their number. I step forward, Sunny still attached, and I'm about to call out when I realize, of course they won't give me anything after I've snapped at them. We'll never sit together in some twinkling dive, in a corner of Philadelphia where the fairy lights are always on, the music so soft it cushions the air, their body solid beside mine, their snide comments slicing the fug of beer. As Minsie vanishes into the conference hall, Sunny's fingers lock around my arm. His crest of hair slumps over his forehead, and I push it back into its cheeky wave. I pick out my car, a charcoal smudge across the lot. Time to go home.

Cheerful Until Next Time

THE QUEER FEMINIST BOOK CLUB CAME TO AN END. Asher sat with the three other members on his rug that looked clean only at night, never under the sharp winter Atlanta sun that pressed down now from the skylight. Brunch debris littered his living room. Dilly, the group's resident English PhD candidate, confirmed what she'd announced at the last meeting: they'd reached the terminus of queer feminist literature, at least that which was available in English. They wouldn't consider—since they couldn't enjoy them together—any unlikely texts penned in Urdu, Hera's native tongue, nor Mandarin or Russian, which Ivan had learned from his father and mother, respectively.

"Are you sure, though?" Ivan asked, picking at the bottom of his shoe, loosening the gravel lodged in the tread. He built a heap of it beside him, carefully arranged, like a mole had tunneled under the carpet.

"There must be more books," said Asher.

Dilly shook her head.

"What about *Away We Fly*?" Ivan asked, winking at him. Asher shivered in delight. Ivan took a special interest in Asher during book club. Mostly, Asher was sure, because Asher was the malest person present. Outside the ecosystem of the meetings, Ivan barely responded to Asher's texts. Ivan would probably reject anyone without a "real" dick. But even if Asher had been assigned male at birth, Ivan, with his boyish face and mischievous mouth, his black flop of hair and long, athletic body, perpetually relaxed in crisply fresh cotton sweaters, would've been miles beyond his league.

"*Away We Fly* is not feminist," Dilly said, fluffing her bushy red ponytail.

"What about *Hegar's Mouth*?" asked Hera. Hera's queerness had not yet manifested but was the subject of speculation among the three other members. Why was she there? In what way could she be queer? This sturdy Pakistani woman, forty at least, the director of some youth program, short and serious and earnest, hair gleaming against her scalp, coiled at the neck like a pretzel.

"Decidedly antifeminist," said Dilly.

"*Anti*feminist?" Asher had loved *Hegar's Mouth*, had been roused by the private world of men he'd hoped to someday join.

"That's ridiculous, Dilly," Ivan said, shaking back his thick hair. "It's a decent choice." If Dilly were to listen to anyone she'd listen to Ivan, who was doing a PhD too, in Political Science.

"If women do not exist in a given world," Dilly said, "that world as we know it is antifeminist. Worse, antiwoman."

"Fine, then," said Hera. "What about *Grim Follies*?"

"Sorry, no." Dilly stretched her soft bluish neck. She

presented as any sassy nerd until you learned she was Atlanta's lesbian Casanova. That's why Hera—ambiguously straight—was the only other girl in book club. Every lesbian in three adjacent zip codes had been through the wringer of a ten-day-average affair with Dilly and in its wake could not be prevailed upon to join.

"It follows a lesbian giantess," Ivan put in. "What's more feminist than that?"

"I didn't say it was antifeminist," Dilly said. "*Grim Follies* is nothing if not feminist. It was engineered by committee for the new feminist audience that was predicted pre-election."

"Don't talk about the election," Ivan said, reaching out a sinewy arm to neaten his gravel pile. "This is the one place we don't talk about the election."

"Then don't bring up *Grim Follies*." Dilly rubbed a dry patch by her mouth, chafing from her latest affair. "*Grim Follies* is inextricable from the election results we thought we'd have."

"But why isn't it a queer feminist text?" Asher asked, though Dilly would shoot down every option. She'd been determined to end the group ever since Rachel, Asher's ex, had moved to Olympia. Perhaps the group was too small to excite Dilly now, or perhaps, without the fun of flirting with Rachel, she no longer cared if they met.

Dilly closed her eyes. "Because it doesn't actively queer anything."

"How can it not?" Hera was flustered. She was the newest member of the group. Dilly and Ivan had run it alone during their undergrad at Brown and their first years at Emory, reading through the canonical works before they recruited Hera, Asher, and Rachel from the Queerlanta subreddit last winter.

"Lesbian giantesses," Ivan said. "Come on. One of them has, like, sex with a tree. Such an epic scene."

Asher snuck him a smile, pushing his jaw out to look manly. Asher wasn't on T. He didn't want to go bald or get cancer and he didn't appreciate facial hair or rough skin. Without it, he rarely passed, even after he'd trained his voice down an octave. Asher's ideal boy-self was sixteen. That was why he kept his hair so shaggy. Ivan requested updates through Asher's transition, which filled Asher with fuzzy warmth. Ever since top surgery two months ago, he was receptive to the excitement, unlike before, when every good thing had been cursed.

"Fantasy can't be queered because it *is* queer, by nature," said Dilly. "All fantasy lit is, like, pre-queered."

Hera bowed her head in defeat. No one knew her well enough to comfort her. If Asher hadn't also been new to the group, he'd have told her not to take Dilly seriously.

"Then I guess this is our last meeting," said Ivan.

"See you shits over the rainbow," said Dilly.

That was exactly what Asher had expected Dilly to say. He'd anticipated this entire evening—Dilly's announcement, the book suggestions. And he was ready with a plan. "Wait," he said as Dilly reached for her keys.

"What?" asked Ivan.

Asher gulped a steadying breath. He was doing this. "There's one last queer feminist text."

"Yeah, right," said Dilly.

"Really. It's called *Cheerful Until Next Time*." The members consulted their phones.

"There's nothing under that title." Ivan shook his phone in a dusty ray of sun. "Besides some like cult band from the eighties."

"I know." Asher pulled a stack of four booklets, rubber-banded together, from his horse-print backpack. "Here are the only copies." He pressed them to his chest, still tender from surgery. He'd been provided antiscarring gel but had only used it once. He cherished the reminder that this body wasn't his birthright.

At a sweltering book club a few weeks earlier, Asher had flaunted his bare chest. Ivan had said his scars looked bad-ass and had asked whether Asher had pictures of his old chest. Asher had tried to joke his way out of it but finally had shared his single photo, snapped minutes before he went under anesthesia, in a panic that he'd forget his old self. Ivan had tipped his head back as though the picture had spat on him. "Shit, dude. That's so not you." He handed the phone back, having already clicked away, cheeks shiny with grati-tude. "What you're doing is amazing." Asher's groin burned. So Ivan did like him. So there was a chance.

"The hell is this?" Dilly turned the slim booklet over in her spidery hands.

"The last queer feminist text in human existence." Asher's heart battered his throat.

"Really?" Dilly narrowed her eyes so the freckles on her eyelids showed.

"Yes," Asher said. "Definitively."

"But it's unpublished," said Dilly.

"Did you write this?" Ivan raised an eyebrow.

"You know I'm not a writer."

Ivan flicked the imageless cover. "*Cheerful Until Next Time.* That's so you though."

Asher's skin tightened. Whatever Ivan meant, at least he was thinking about Asher.

"Make a case for this, Asher, sweetie," Dilly said. "Before we waste our time on some zine."

"It's not a zine," Asher said. "It's one continuous piece. Full of mysteries, riddles, and the stuff of life."

Ivan honked out a genuine laugh. Dilly peeled open the first page.

"Stop," Asher said. "Don't read it."

"Why?" Mercifully, Dilly let the volume snap shut.

Sweat stuck in Asher's hairline. He'd been certain the intrigue of the booklet would suffice. Who wouldn't be curious about the fifteen folded pages, bound with covers cut from grocery bags, the interior typed and stapled up the spine, still reeking of photocopier ink? Asher had printed it in the department late at night, when the administrator wouldn't poke in and awkwardly flirt—proving she was progressive by accepting him as male. All the time he'd formatted and copied and folded and stapled, he'd imagined Ivan reading it and falling in love. "It's not the kind of thing you want to read around other people."

"You mean it's sexually explicit?" Dilly asked, in her favorite sultry voice.

"More than you can imagine," said Asher. "Now I gotta kick you guys out. I have class prep." He couldn't stand it if the group thumbed through the booklets in front of him, Dilly reading a line out loud, Hera chuckling. And Ivan—no. His plan could only work if Ivan absorbed the content alone.

Once the group was gone, Asher rattled around, stacking paper plates and wadding napkins. The apartment felt oversized and empty now, especially in bleak midafternoon, as he finished out the last months of his two-year rhetoric fellowship, coaxing freshmen to write essays they should've learned to draft in high school. Rachel had left him in the fall, and it hadn't made sense to move. Now it was another overwarm January, bare trees fighting for respect against the flip-flops slapping the slopes of Druid Hills. Atlanta's mild climate had eased Asher's breakup. At least he had the sun, or whatever.

He halfheartedly swept around Ivan's molehill of gravel. He always let the pile be until the day he inevitably stepped in it on the way to the bathroom. The gravel then scattered everywhere, and he scooped it up and stowed it in the least popular mug in the cupboard.

Rachel had hated that mug. She'd loved Asher like no

parent had ever loved him, but she'd also picked at him like a parent: for letting dust thicken on his books, for brushing his teeth too loudly, for resting his ass on the kitchen counter. For saving gravel. He'd thought he'd be relieved when she was gone, but his chest ached like his heart had been removed, collateral damage from the mastectomy.

At first he'd thought the breakup was due to his transition. She'd been cool with the idea in theory, all the way until his surgery was scheduled. But as she'd packed to leave him, still butchering pronouns months into his social transition, he'd read her diary, desperate to uncover why she was really leaving. The entry revealed that she'd known about Asher's crush, had suspected the real reason their sex life had shrunk from glorified masturbation to nothing: *I hate her sometimes, Jesus. I thought she was just a slob but last night she was staring at that stupid mug of gravel like she was in love with it, like I'm not even here. She was, like, practically coming all over that gravel. Does she think I'm an idiot? I mean he, whatever. It's like he thinks Ivan left a pile of dirt as a gift—so delusional. Ashley would fuck anyone who soils our rug. Anyone but me. I hate that I'm crying right now. Why do I still care?*

In handwriting shaky with shock, she'd scrawled over these words the insult that became the acronym for Asher's booklet title. And despite the insult's nastiness—though the femininity was worse—she'd written it in a curly script better reserved for wedding invitations. Asher had photographed the entry with his phone, barely managing to slip the diary back into its box before Rachel burst into the room, face tight with the false lawyerly cheer that propelled her through the breakup.

Besides the rants about Asher's crush, the entry contained surprisingly sweet projections about Asher's transition: the pain of his forthcoming surgery, the childhood nicknames he'd abandon, the awkwardness of running into people who'd mistake him for a cousin of his former self. *This is so dubious, this transition bullshit, like what the fuck is she doing? I'm not even breathing right now. I'm, like, sick. Because how can I promise to love some boy I've never met? But then I look at him and I'm, like, some parts will stay, right? I can focus my love on the parts that will stay. Like his mouse nose, that silly hair. I love her so much it's stupid.*

Months later, propelled by Dilly's growing disinterest in the club, Asher had typed and printed the four-page diary entry, preparing the booklet as his grand gesture. When Ivan read it, he'd understand that Asher's crush was serious. He'd see how much Rachel had loved him, how lovable he was. How, even in her anger, she'd hated to lose him.

As Asher scurried around wiping grease off the stove, his phone rang with its festive buzzing birds. Ivan's face appeared on the screen. Asher tossed the device, having forgotten he'd programmed in Ivan's photograph, which had clearly not been taken consensually: depicting Ivan chomping an egg burrito that Asher had folded for him at a book club meeting back in August. Asher had already appreciated, by then, the way Ivan moved like liquid, curled on the floor leaning against Asher's rock-hard couch, not flinching when a cockroach paused to nibble a tablet of poison.

"Let him eat," Asher had said. "He'll share it with his family and they'll all die."

Ivan had rolled his eyes like he was Asher's brother or like they'd been boys together. Asher had longed to flirt back. Instead he'd squeezed Rachel's hand.

Asher found his phone in the corner of the room and hit ignore. He needed Ivan to finish reading, to let the text absorb. He paced to his rickety coffee table and back. The phone rang again. Ivan, again. If only Asher's past self could see him hitting ignore on the call he'd yearned for months to receive. He would burn off his nerves by walking to Emory Village for coffee.

Outside, the January afternoon was summery and calm, the sky a white blanket of sun. Cedar waxwings picked at glossy berries hanging over the stoop. As Asher stepped onto the gravel walkway, Dilly burst from a shrub. She screamed, puffs of ginger hair jangling, her face wrenched in eager horror.

"Oh god." Asher was embarrassed to find his hand on his heart. He touched his chest often since the surgery, reminding himself that he finally had what he'd long needed.

"Ha!" she cried.

"What, have you been here since the meeting?"

"I knew that book was fishy. And holy shit." Her face lit up. "Asher. You said you didn't write it."

He took a breath. Here, it started. "I didn't say that. I said I'm not a writer."

"That's effectively the same thing."

"No it's not, Little Miss Semantics."

"Are you sure you want to do this? I mean, Asher. You gave it to the whole group."

"I'm not going to give it to just one of you, am I?"

"One of us." She stuck her fist to her hip. "So you *do* love him."

He wasn't surprised that she wasn't surprised. Dilly may have been Phi Beta Kappa and a Rhodes Scholar and on an endowed fellowship at Emory, but her kicks came from crushes and entanglements. While he was still with Rachel, he'd been subtle about his feelings for Ivan. But, post-breakup, he changed tactics. Ivan hadn't noticed, so why should Asher care if Dilly did? Maybe Dilly wanted to end the group because she was jealous of Asher and Ivan's connection, the way they'd stolen off together to look at Asher's photo.

"So?" he asked.

"So? You're a lesbian, Asher."

He scowled. "No, I'm not."

"Basically, yeah." She swung her arms in the sunshine. "Tits and pronouns aside."

"Get out of here." Dilly had never hit on Asher, even when he was living as a girl. Wasn't that proof enough he wasn't one?

"Look." She flipped open the booklet. "*His name was Ashley,*" she read.

"Dilly." Dilly was her queer name, gifted by an older

Midtown butch. Dilly was not a name that lent itself to desperate pleas.

"*Which is a man's name, remember,*" Dilly read on, chin up, hair catching light in its curls. "*But not enough so he'd keep it. He's vain about losing that stupid name, whining about how beautiful it is. Ashley, Ashley. He whispers it sometimes when he thinks he's alone.*" She crumpled her nose. "You think that's how you'll win him? Do you even know Ivan?"

The truth was, Asher might not win Ivan. They only saw each other monthly at book club, after all. But Ivan asked him so often about his transition, seemed so sweetly invested, that he must've been interested. And Asher had already tried everything else. He hadn't won Ivan by staring at him during meetings, or by texting him at two in the morning, or by studying critiques of the books they read so he'd have the sharpest comments. He hadn't won Ivan by wanting him, all the time, even back a year ago when Rachel lay next to him in bed. He hadn't won him by Googling him in secret and raising topics that might appeal—hockey, because Ivan had played as a kid; Dungeons and Dragons, ditto; Wisconsin, because he'd lived there; beer and cheese, because of Wisconsin; felony riots, because he'd been charged with one, years ago, at the Republican National Convention in Saint Paul and his mug shot was still posted, way down the results. He was so hot in that mug shot, with his crew cut, and his shoulders sagging, holding the placard like it weighed days. So if none of that had worked, then what? Then this piece of writing that was more intimate than anything he'd ever written himself.

"*Soon those beautiful breasts will be gone*," Dilly continued. "*Such a fucking waste. They'll be ghost breasts jiggling through the sky. At least he's not on T yet. At least he doesn't have a pedophile's mustache.* Blah blah blah. Yeah, we know. You boring transkids are always yammering about logistics."

Asher hated the sound of *breasts*. The hissing close of the word, the yeasty opening, still sickened him, even now that he had none to claim.

"*Asher loves Ivan. It's obvious. Though first he wanted to be him.*"

Asher had been shocked when he read that line. That Rachel had known Asher deeply enough to understand he'd wanted to *be* Ivan first, wanted the cold course of Siberian blood cooling his organs, deleting the pads of fat over his hips and belly, melting the soft patches where his chest used to be, shaving down his cheeks until the hard edges of his skull pushed at his skin like Ivan's. Asher stopped the thought—he shouldn't exoticize, he was disgusting. He slammed his hip with his open palm to jar himself back to logic.

"And how, may I ask, is this exactly feminist?" Dilly asked. "It's all about dudes."

Asher raised his chin. "Except for the author."

"I thought you were still denying your female side."

Dilly insisted that, since Asher's transition was not "complete," he was still partly female and should retain that portion of his identity for political reasons. Asher argued that he could be a man—actually, he preferred boy (at thirty he still passed for twelve)—any way he wanted. Having studied Gender and Sexuality in undergrad didn't grant her license to police him.

"I didn't write it," Asher said.

"But look," Dilly said. "*His name was Ashley.* That's you. Just in the weird-ass third person."

"No," said Asher. "That's Rachel."

Dilly's mouth slackened. "Rachel Rachel?"

Dilly had been impressed, as everyone was, by how beautiful Rachel was, with her auburn curls and beaky mouth, her torso a slender curve, and especially by the fancy academic law positions she secured wherever she went—New Haven, Boston, Atlanta, where she'd received a cushy law review fellowship, and now Olympia. Dilly had mocked Asher for letting her go: "Why didn't you pass her to me? I could handle a girl like that."

Dilly bowed back into the text, receiving it with new knowledge. The pages were so nakedly written, so humiliating in their awkwardness, that Asher had thought at first he'd written them himself, or that Rachel had tapped into his thought stream. *He paces the apartment like an animal. He's sick of it all—me, especially. Sometimes I find him clenching like he's trying to shit, like he's willing himself gone.*

She'd scooped out a teaspoon of his most secret emotions. He went woozy picturing Ivan reading those words, understanding Asher's transition in the most intimate way possible. Learning Asher was thoughtful and lovable, that the two of them had potential for more than a hookup, a filling up of each other's loneliest pockets.

Dilly lowered the pages. "Man," she said. "Rachel doesn't look too awesome here. Did she give you permission to share this?"

"Yes," Asher lied. He wouldn't entertain the antifeminist implications of sharing without Rachel's consent. And it wasn't like the whole text was flattering to Asher, either. A nasty nugget crouched at the center: *I'm fucking beautiful. Whatever, I can say it here He should want me. But instead he has to be this cliché. He's not even on T, so why does he like a man? Because it's trendy? He never has before.* That was true, but not every crush was a referendum on sexuality. He'd probably like women again. Why not? *Or because he's fucking racist, I bet. I bet he thinks Ivan's kind of feminine because he's half Chinese. He thinks being with Ivan will essentially be like being with a woman.* Asher had thrown the journal across the room the first time he read that passage, bile jumping into his throat. When he retrieved the journal, pinching it by the very corner like it was infectious, the words blurred and refocused. They were really there, printed in ink. Rachel had written those words about Asher, about Ivan. He clutched his stomach as it churned. She was wrong. He didn't think that way. He was sure he didn't. But wouldn't he be a hypocrite to cut that part? Wasn't every white person racist, in the end?

"That's so messed up." Dilly rattled the pages. "Rachel has integrity, Asher."

"She won't find out." Distributing the pages made him feel close to Rachel. Like they were united again in a mutual goal. If you forgot that goal was getting him laid by someone else.

"The only reason I don't think you're a total turd right now is this is so you. Like she stole it from you in the first place."

There were only a few errors. Like *breasts*, and her overestimation of his frequency of masturbation and underestimation of how much he loved her. "Don't tell anyone."

Dilly winced. "You're crazy." Her arms wheeled around. "This is one of those crazy things people do for love, like moving in with a married polyamorous sub they met on Insta."

"No, it's not." Though he liked the idea of setting down a duffel bag in Ivan's loft.

Dilly stepped back, both hands on the booklet. "Asher. Are you sure?" She spoke in an unfamiliar low tone: "You know, this doesn't make you look very appealing either."

"That's the whole point. I'm making myself vulnerable." He led her down the walkway to the road. What did he have left to offer but his true self, worms included?

"I don't know, Asher."

His head filled with the cool steam of rage. Like all those years living as a girl, everyone forever telling him he didn't know what he wanted. He didn't want ice cream so early in the day. He didn't want to teach in the South. He didn't want to be a guy, really, did he? When he was so nice-looking as a girl? They only ever said nice-looking. They never said pretty.

As Dilly stepped forward, arms out for a hug, he backed up toward his building. "You need to leave."

Once she was gone, he checked his phone. Ivan again, face and burrito blinking across the screen. This time, Asher answered. "Just come over." He hung up.

Trembling, he forced himself to relax by sitting on the couch, but his back was stiff against the cushions. What could Dilly have meant? Was the booklet unflattering because he was so in love with Ivan that it was pathetic? Or because he'd stolen the words from Rachel, which was obvious after a careful read? Or because Ivan would learn too much about Asher's transition and see Asher as a girl? But Ivan had known Asher a year, since back when he'd lived as female. He'd been sweet about Asher's transition. That was how he let his interest show. Asher shouldn't have used Rachel's words. But Rachel would want him to be happy, wouldn't she?

And besides, he hadn't only used the nice parts. He'd included the worst passage ever written about himself. For weeks he'd ignored that portion of the entry, too pained to so much as glance at it. Maybe Rachel was racist herself and had projected her feelings onto him. She'd been jealous of Ivan, and her rage had come out sideways in words he covered with his finger when he was brave enough to revisit the entry.

But slowly, over weeks, Asher realized that, if he was being honest with himself, he *had* entertained the thought, if half-submerged, that part of his crush on Ivan was related to Ivan's pretty face and girlier manner. Though he'd never consciously connected those features to Ivan's race. He'd considered removing that bit when he made the booklet—or adding a caveat—but decided, rashly, to leave the entry intact. Ivan was brilliant. He'd appreciate Asher's radical honesty, his vulnerability. In these new political times, white people couldn't walk around anymore pretending they were free of racism. If you admitted your flawed thinking, then at least you were wrestling, in some small way, with all that was wrong with the world. And during book club discussions, Ivan had appreciated when Asher mentioned white supremacy or his own limitations as a white reader. He'd be impressed by Asher's self-awareness.

An hour after Dilly left, the doorbell rang. Asher floated to answer it as if compelled. Behind the door stood Ivan, his shoes sunk in gravel. That lovely face—thin but solid, built to sustain good looks through abusive Siberian winters—distorted into a smirk.

"Hi," said Asher, the syllable a hard ding on the air.

Ivan entered the apartment. They'd never hung out one-on-one. Asher's skin buzzed—did Ivan like him? Was he horrified? Was this the beginning of a relationship or the end of a friendship? Or both? He forgot to worry about the mess: towers of paper plates, bagel skins hollowed out and hardening into dried rings.

Asher followed Ivan into the living room. He looked

away from the denim-clad butt peeking from under Ivan's Christmas-red sweater, but he had to notice it was shapely and sweet.

The air was dense, and Asher forced his way through it. Ivan sat on the couch and Asher sat in the desk chair. During book club, no one ever sat on the couch or in the desk chair. Since there weren't enough real seats, no one indulged.

"I figured out why Hera's queer." Ivan's voice was so flat it barely traveled.

"Really?" Asher tried to fill the room with his exuberance. "That's amazing. Why?"

"She's asexual, aromantic, and pansexual."

"What?" Asher cried, barking a false laugh. "That's like a punchline." But Ivan wasn't smiling. "I guess she earned her spot?"

Ivan grimaced. "I feel bad. She confided in me."

Sour dripped into Asher's throat. Was this Ivan's way of telling him he was embarrassed by Asher's confession? "Are you okay?"

"Look." Ivan leaned back against the couch. "Asher. I read your booklet thing." Ivan slid the booklet halfway out of his pocket. It was so vulgar looking, the raw paper naked in the open air.

Asher gripped the upholstered seat. "Yeah?"

"There's a lot to say. I love—let's see." He took a strained breath. "I guess I love this pre-election hope you have. Like all this nuance about trans issues that's disappeared now that people are afraid."

Asher squeezed his fist. "I thought we weren't supposed to discuss the election."

"We're not in a meeting now."

"So what is this?"

"I suppose that depends whether or not you want to be with a woman."

"What?"

"Well. I assumed this booklet was your way of hitting on me."

"Yeah." The word caught in Asher's throat. "I mean, I guess, yeah. It was."

"So don't be a pussy. If you want to be with me, it's going to be like being with a woman, right?" He flipped open the booklet. "Like you wrote: *being with Ivan will essentially be like being with a woman.*"

Out loud, the words sounded foul. Worse than foul, cruel. And he couldn't suddenly say, *Just joking! I didn't write that!* A breath jerked up in his throat, but what croaked out was, "Why are you attacking me?"

"I'm giving you the benefit of the doubt."

Asher leaned his head against the wall. The cool of the plaster spread through him. He couldn't connect to the solidity of his building, couldn't assure himself it would still be here when Ivan left, which he was surely about to do. "You forced me to show you that picture," he said. So Asher had been bad, awful. But so had Ivan—at least a little.

Ivan's eyes rolled up, as though searching for what Asher

meant. Then his face sharpened. "I asked your permission about that. You were eager enough to share."

Asher crossed his arms over his chest. "I felt gross."

"Asher. Come on."

Asher was in the wrong. He should back down. But his throat thickened. "I'm weird about my body. You're so interested in my transition, you should know that." This wasn't fair. He understood being treated badly by the world. He'd changed his whole gender, after all.

"I'm sorry." Ivan's face went gray. "But that's not what we're talking about."

Asher leaped to his feet. His muscles vibrated—he had to defend himself, what could he say? But every rebuttal he marshaled would only make him sound fragile. Ivan stood too, and they hovered side-by-side in the center of the room. Asher had never realized before that he was taller than Ivan—barely, but he was. They'd always been sitting down or too far apart in the kitchen preparing food. The springy whorl on top of Ivan's head was childish, a cheeky rude cowlick.

Without moving, they were somehow closer. Ivan touched Asher's hip, leaving an electric handprint. Asher's eyes slid closed as he waited for the kiss. Because, of course, a kiss was the only way to erase the conversation. The feeling was of such inevitability that he wasn't even excited. Of course a kiss was next.

But Ivan circled around Asher and drew down his sweatpants, the elastic waistband catching as it dragged along the length of Asher's legs. Why was Asher wearing sweatpants at the most important crossroads of his life? But his muscles relaxed when Ivan set his hands on Asher's naked skin, heated by the skylight and Ivan's breath, steady and slow, directly behind him. Sunshine shone straight through Asher. Their romance was starting, finally. Asher's ass was out. He was forgiven. If it were Asher's choice, he'd kiss first—it was creepy standing here half-naked—and he had to stifle an urge to turn his head and catch Ivan's lips. But if he shifted at all, he might startle Ivan away. Best to wait for Ivan's move.

Ivan held his ass so firmly that if he let go, Asher would collapse. Was Asher clean enough? Was his ass too feminine? He bent at the waist. He clenched his teeth, preparing for Ivan's dick. But then there was the splash of Ivan's mouth, landing wetly with deadly aim.

Asher twitched in surprise. They were starting like this, okay. Ivan's tongue ran all the way up Asher's crack and he bit his mouth not to scream. He could bear the licking a minute more, maybe, thirty seconds. The act was a promise. No one tasted anyone's ass if they weren't into that person. Right? He bargained with himself—one more wet stroke of the tongue, then he'd turn and hug Ivan, tell him how much he cared. Two more strokes. Three. That was all he had to withstand. But somehow, Ivan's tongue morphed, turning sparky and sharp. He flooded with liquid warmth. He shut his eyes, his torso moving in a slow wave. But then the question jolted through him: Why had Ivan chosen his ass? He was interacting with the most gender-neutral part of Asher's body. Of course: he couldn't bear to face Asher's other parts. He was sickened by them.

Ivan pushed deeper now, faster, pumping relentlessly. Asher's anus, the whole area, went raw, screaming. But he'd wanted Ivan so long. And they were friends. Then why was Ivan moving so mechanically? Ivan's hands shaped Asher's edges, emphasizing his curves. Asher folded his arms over his chest the way he always had before surgery, protecting what was long gone.

He bit his tongue, but he couldn't block a cry. He sounded like an animal, like a girl, and he wanted to stuff the sound back down his throat, to suffocate himself with it. He pulled away.

Ivan stood up. Asher looked away from his mouth, afraid to see it soiled. He jerked up his pants. What was that, even? Why hadn't Ivan stopped? Why hadn't Asher stopped him? After the booklet, maybe Ivan knew Asher didn't have the right.

Ivan looked flushed, despondent, like he'd vanished from his body.

Asher's anus tingled, soggy and embarrassed. He pulled up his sweatpants. "I didn't mean to write about you that way. Like, as girly or whatever. I wasn't serious."

Ivan's head cocked on his slender neck. "Yes, you were."

Asher's shoulders went leaden. He shrugged.

Ivan's face was slack now, relaxed. "It's okay, man," he said. But it wasn't.

•

The book club never met again. Asher never saw Ivan again, intentionally. Once, though, a year or so later, Asher was crossing the liberal arts quad at Emory, when, several hundred feet away, Ivan emerged from his department, heading on quick feet in the opposite direction. Instead of his normal clothes, he wore high-waisted girls' pants that hugged his thighs, a cropped sweater, and a soft pink shawl. His hair was still short, his gait still boyish.

Asher hurried to catch up, pushing past undergraduates cameled by backpacks, skirting a table offering lollypops on behalf of mental illness. If he could glimpse Ivan's face, he'd understand who Ivan was now. But after circling a clump of girls lodged in a group hug, the quad cleared. Ivan was gone.

In the years that follow, still in the same apartment, adjuncting now, Asher wonders whether it matters if Ivan also transitioned, whether Asher's terrible thoughts were justified because he spotted a quality in Ivan that was already there. But that's no excuse for how he acted. He'd wrestled with his assumptions and lost.

Now sometimes he soothes himself, alone in his apartment, swirling Ivan's gravel in the mug. He tastes it, sometimes, as punishment, as though Ivan could see him rolling the debris across his tongue, forcing the sharp grit against the enamel of his molars. Like Ivan would care anyway. The gesture is childish. By now enough time has passed that he's sucked all the dirt off, and the gravel is as clean as salt.

Ooh, the Suburbs

As soon as Heidi arrived at Kim's condo, she suggested they go meet LisaParsonsTwo, Kim's online crush. Usually Kim was the rule-breaker, the wild girl whose mom let her do whatever, but Heidi had obsessed over LisaParsonsTwo since Kim had told her about their messages last week. Kim's mom was out for the evening, so Heidi had invited herself to sleep over.

"You don't want hot dogs?" Kim brandished the package. She'd let it sit out way too long—the protective ice had dissolved and the meat was pale and clammy. Kim pinched a puckered end and winked.

Heidi slit her eyes. "What's wrong with you? She's your crush. Of course you want to go." Heidi would fluff Kim back up to her normal self, that cool, slouchy tomboy. "And you never cook."

"I thought it was a nice night to stay in and enjoy dogs. I have mayonnaise."

"Kim. Come on. There's so much buildup."

"I thought you wanted a fun night in." Kim flapped the

hot dogs, puffing meaty air toward Heidi. "Just me and you. Like old times."

Heidi smoothed her flyaway hair. She was thirteen but looked eleven and was pushed around all the time. She liked this new feeling of freaking someone out—especially Kim, who was the daring one. Who'd found this mysterious on-line woman in the first place. Heidi needed to go to Boston tonight, needed to watch Kim bravely charm an adult woman, so that, one day, she could flirt with one herself. She took a breath. "You mean you're chicken."

"Not really." Kim's bottom lip popped out.

"You think you're so tough," Heidi said. "But you're not, are you?"

Though they'd been best friends for nearly a year, Heidi had never spoken to Kim so boldly. She stepped forward, molding a face of intimidation. Kim rolled her eyes but said, "Fine, whatever you want," and shuffled into the shadows to make arrangements on AIM. Heidi loomed over her as Kim typed with one hand, massaging her hot dogs with the other.

Heidi couldn't still her heart as they stepped into the snowy night, passing the decorative rock engraved with the name of the apartment complex—Stony Court—and crossing the parking lot toward Mass Ave. Ever since Kim had first mentioned LisaParsonsTwo, Heidi had lain in bed each night imagining their correspondence: the bleak white dialogue box, filled alternately with Kim's blue screen name and Lisa Parsons's red screen name. Kim had been vague about what they discussed, but Heidi was certain their chats brimmed with eroticism and romance. She'd begged Kim to let her see, but Kim had called her a certified perv and only shared choice quotes. Tonight Kim's seduction skills would finally be on view. Heidi was so sick of her dreary life, mildewing into antique rugs at her dad's house, laboring over math worksheets.

"Don't let that woman drive you anywhere," Heidi's father had said of Kim's mom, Nancy. "Not even to the corner store. And if she starts in on the marijuana, tell her your father doesn't like funny business. If she doesn't listen, step into another room. Then call 911."

Kim and Heidi trudged through the snow, which was stale, yellow foam under the fresh marshmallow layer. Heidi turned back to check the light in Kim's living room on the second floor. If Heidi hadn't pressed for the trip, they'd be in there now, her finger filling a burn hole in the couch, hearing secrets from Kim's old school: how she'd masturbated under her desk during social studies; how she'd seduced her resource room teacher; how she'd skimmed her mother's marijuana, a fistful at a time, and secured it in the belly of her hippo bank. Heidi was done with hearing about Kim's experiences. She was ready to be out in the world witnessing them.

"You'll seduce LisaParsonsTwo, right?" Heidi asked.

"Doy," said Kim. "I'll seduce her so hard."

As they reached Mass Ave., Heidi zipped her puffy jacket, frail armor against the winter night. "How far is the bus stop?"

"This is the bus stop," Kim said. "Are you blind?"

They hunched in the shelter, where snow blew in sideways. Kim's chunky black pixie cut collected a dusting, like powdered sugar on chocolate cake. Her breasts formed a shelf for the snow, the cotton of her sweatshirt darkening as flakes melted from her heat.

"How do we get to Beacon Hill?" Heidi asked. The name sounded like a lighthouse at the center of the city, beaming a path to safe harbor.

"Doy." Kim brushed snow off her hair. "Seventy-six to Alewife, Alewife to Park Street, then walk or take the Green Line to Government Center."

"Cool," Heidi said, and then, though she'd never been, "I love Government Center."

"Ew, why? Hey, do you think anyone will die in this storm?"

"No chance. Everyone clears their tailpipes now."

During the last snowstorm a local couple had died in their car, late at night, waiting for their windows to defrost. Their tailpipe had become clogged with snow. They'd lost themselves talking, the newspaper thought, hadn't noticed they were drifting off, maybe confused the feeling with love. Heidi obsessed over the woman dying first, her bowed head enticing the man into his own coma. They'd met through HistoryBuffSingles.net, and the *Lexington Minuteman* had excerpted their personals. It was wrong they'd died just when they'd found each other. They'd both listed the Hundred Years' War, Rice-A-Roni, and human tenderness as interests.

The couple's death was the singularly most compelling story Heidi had encountered.

Kim leaned against the shelter post and flipped her hood up. God, if only Heidi could be Kim. She scared herself by acting like her father: washing her hands three times after using bleach, removing the hair dryer from the bathroom in case it slipped into the tub while she was bathing, quizzing Nancy on the location and condition of the carbon monoxide detector. Kim was the only exciting feature of her life; Kim, whose mom smoked cloves and wore silk scarves wrapped around her neck like bandages. Kim, who used to live by the ocean, who visited the city after dark, who'd come out as a lesbian in fourth grade.

Last year, soon after they met, Kim came out to Heidi. They were sharing a cushion on Kim's floor, and Heidi asked, "But how do you know? Everyone has fantasies." In a discussion about President Clinton, her dad had told her that fantasies are for the mind alone. That if you want to think of someone who acts on fantasies, you should think of a serial killer.

"I just know." Kim worried the frayed edge of the mat. "I get boobs and boobs get me. What fantasies do you have?"

Mean bosses filled Heidi's mind. Female bosses. And, though she'd be humiliated if anyone ever knew, moms. Moms who knew better but couldn't help themselves. Moms with shaggy hair and graceful limbs. "I guess Greg Luce is cute."

That's when Kim started in on her stories from Scituate, which Heidi pictured as a cheerful cluster of brown buildings pressed against the Atlantic, though her dad insisted it was a second-rate town with a dangerously defective sewage system. In Scituate, Kim had dated a popular girl named Kelly Stephanie.

Kim obviously knew Heidi was gay too, though they'd never discussed it. She gave a funny smile when she caught Heidi studying accidentally homoerotic advertisements, like two women plunging their hands into a bowl of popcorn, blue TV light on their skin, pajamaed legs tucked under their hips. The idea of two adult women in a living room at night swept Heidi's head from her shoulders.

Maybe Heidi should become secret girlfriends with Kim, as the whole school assumed anyway. But her feelings for Kim ranged only from tepid satisfaction to fierce affection, the normal range of feelings for a platonic companion.

"What will Lisa Parsons be like?" Heidi asked. "Do you think that's her real name?"

"It's probably a pseudonym." Kim crushed a circle into the snow. "Probably her name is Beef Jessica or something."

"Why would her pseudonym be more normal than her regular name?"

"Why do you care?" Kim's eyes glinted, challenging.

"Of course I care. You're my best friend."

"You're not *my* best friend."

Heidi frowned. "Well, who is?"

"My pussy." Kim laughed wildly, then shoved Heidi with two hands.

Heidi collapsed backward and the snow accepted her with cold, wet arms. Kim pounced on her and stuffed her leg between Heidi's, mashing her crotch.

"I'm going to beat you," Kim said.

Heidi gasped, willing herself to ignore the burn between her legs, the sweetness of the friction. They wrestled all the time under Kim's black light posters: wild, grasping fights that led to a pop of pleasure so deep it hurt. Tonight the snow made the whole world private. Even the air was white, so bright that the snowflakes danced gray against it.

Heidi hooked her chin over Kim's shoulder to avoid eye contact. Together, they pressed the snow down with their weight, sinking their platform, until rocks and the trash of summer poked Heidi's spine.

"Pretend I'm Greg Luce," Kim said.

Heidi pretended Kim was the black-haired woman laminated on the shelter wall, with a sharp nose and crow's-feet, passing kibble to a Pekingese. The woman's hands stroked Heidi's hips as she spoke in low, firm tones, Heidi raging all over.

As Heidi pressed closer to Kim, her thighs and butt numbing against the cold, the woman on the poster blurring into peach and black and green, even the Pekingese becoming erotic, with its long, fleshy body, they were hit with floodlights.

Heidi pushed Kim off so hard that she crashed onto her side, her mouth filling with snow.

"Chill out," Kim said, spitting slush. "Why else would we be here?"

As the bus pulled up, Heidi leaped onboard. But when she faced the driver—bearded, raw-eyed—it was obvious he'd seen her grappling with Kim. His chin was set. "Girls?" he said.

She couldn't tell what he was asking, so she paid and took her seat. As the bus lurched forward, she studied the strip of greenish skin and shiny eyes in the rearview. Had he thought she and Kim were fighting, as they always claimed they were? Kim's mom, Nancy, might know she and Kim messed around. "Kim's lucky to have you," she'd said once.

The driver's eyelids sagged over his pupils. Heidi turned and squashed her face against the freezing window.

The coffee shop where they'd arranged to meet LisaParsons-Two was a sandstone block of a building on a hill above Boston Common. A metalwork sign, PECULIAR TREATS, wrought in cursive, hung over the door. With a trembling hand, Kim squeezed a roll of belly and jammed it into her jeans. She smeared cola-flavored ChapStick throughout her hair, lifting her bangs to expose the confetti of whiteheads on her forehead. She claimed the smell of cola made girls horny, that cocktail of tang, caramel, and caffeine.

"Ready?" Heidi bounced on her heels, eager to get inside. "Do you know your first come-ons?"

Kim rubbed her waxy fingers on Heidi's shoulder. "Or

we could just hang out, you and me. Like walk around the Common. Find a hot dog stand."

Heidi took a breath. "Let's check this place out. Since we're here."

Inside, a blue-haired girl worked the counter, jelly bracelets bouncing as she foamed milk. Men sat on stools, or they might've been stone butches, which Kim had once described as lesbians with off-limits boobs.

"Where's Lisa?" Heidi whispered.

"How am I supposed to know?" Kim twitched like a squirrel.

"Fix your hair." A gob of ChapStick had lodged in Kim's bangs. She scraped at it distractedly. "Are you even ready?"

"Doy," Kim said, her voice a ghost.

Each step downstairs was danker than the last, the air cold and dense and mildewed. The basement was split into chambers by wall hangings and strings of lights tossed over pipes. The walls were padded with animal-patterned rugs, screen-printed sheets softening the surfaces: desert landscapes, clouds piled over ponds, geese arranged in formal units in the sky. A group of women huddled together, older than the high schoolers who smoked on Ledgelawn and younger than the parents whisking by in wood-paneled minivans. The age of no one in the suburbs. The smallest one had rolled her hair into twigs. Another wore a bandanna and overalls, feathers dripping from her earlobes. One had balls studded along the curl of her ear, like a wolf tagged for research. Heidi's favorite was a large woman—older than the rest—with bleary cow eyes and a silk shirt that reached her knees, peacocks glittering from the billowing fabric. Her hands tickled her thighs like nervous spiders. She looked like she'd pull a runaway in from the cold or stroke a stray. Unlike Heidi's father, who was too afraid of fleas to help anyone.

The woman watched Heidi, cheeks brightening. "Kim?"

"Lisa?" Lisa Parsons was at least twenty-five. But she didn't look repulsed by the girls at the threshold, not even by Heidi's puffy coat, sagging jeans, and gum boots. In fact, she seemed to prefer Heidi, carefully scanning her over.

Lisa Parsons stood up on tiny feet. "I didn't expect you to be two."

"I'm not Kim." Heidi turned to Kim, rolling her hand in signal for her to begin her seduction. Kim just stood there, feet planted in the carpet.

"Ah." Lisa Parsons turned to the real Kim. "Nice to meet you, Kim. I've enjoyed our chats."

"Yeah." Kim teetered where she stood. Why wasn't she dashing forward to begin the great romance of her life?

Lisa Parsons blushed. "Would you care to meet my friends?" Women from the group watched on, some with lattes pressed to their cheeks, some flashing blocky teeth.

"Fine." Kim spoke so loudly that Lisa Parsons turned to Heidi, startled.

"And what's your name?"

"Um, Heidi?"

"Is that German?" a lesbian asked. "Guten Tag, Umheidi."

Lisa Parsons offered them a corduroy couch, low-slung

like a beanbag. Heidi squeezed past the coffee table and claimed the middle. Kim perched on the armrest by the door, her body tipped toward the exit.

"Everybody." Lisa Parsons spread her hands. "Meet Heidi and Kim, my mentees from the internet."

Heidi splashed with heat at being placed on equal footing with Kim.

"Aw," cooed the twig-haired woman, resting her bejeweled hand on the lesbian beside her. "Lisa's so generous with the baby bears. You girls don't even know she's been working with gay youth for, what, three years?"

"Five." Lisa Parsons blushed at the carpet.

"She was at BAGLY, but these days she finds kids on her own, helps them out big time." The twig-haired woman twisted one twig punishingly tight. "What do you call it, Lisa?"

"Personal mentorship," Lisa Parsons said, watching Kim and Heidi.

Looming over the girls, Lisa Parsons's proud pancake face almost passed for professional. And maybe Kim could imagine someone was in love with her when all they wanted was to help gay youth. But Kim had quoted chats where Lisa Parsons made reference to acts more intimate than Kim and Heidi's fighting. Once, Heidi had reeled to the bathroom, overwhelmed.

Lisa Parsons offered Heidi her latte. Heidi took a sip, then flooded her mouth with spit to dilute the heat. "The flavor of heaven," she said. Maybe she wouldn't have to wait for the next mysterious woman. If Kim wasn't interested, Lisa

Parsons could be Heidi's chance. Why not? Bitter milk dribbled into her throat.

The women discussed vegetarian marshmallows and a menstruation aid called the Keeper. Heidi could take the train here every day after school. She'd claim she'd gotten into a play, but really she'd be perched on Lisa Parsons's knee, laughing with everyone but pausing to whisper in Lisa Parsons's ear a private jest or special memory.

"What's your favorite subject, Kim?" Lisa Parsons asked.

"Math?"

"She means English," Heidi said.

"What do you like about English?"

"This is stupid"—Heidi pitched her voice deeper—"but sometimes we give the books new plots." Heidi loved the days they spent on Kim's floor, Nancy at work or out with friends, sounding off without filter. Scout murdered Dill, Holden Caulfield grew up to become a Broadway producer. The kids in *Lord of the Flies* hitched a ride on a Disney Cruise.

"I was creative too, once," Lisa Parsons said. "Sometimes I wonder how I ended up in medicine."

"You work in medicine?" Heidi scooted to the edge of the cushion. Out in the world, she could meet people in any profession, not just the same batch of fools at the same dumb school. She yearned for every detail of Lisa Parsons's life: the meat smell on the tiles in her hospital, her apartment with a brown velvet couch and portraits of friends pinned to the refrigerator, the freedom to go out and walk the city any time of night. That's how bonds formed.

"Kim, you didn't tell Heidi about my job?"

"Don't remember."

Lisa Parsons blinked with hurt. Maybe Kim was disappointed with Lisa Parsons's weight or age. The picture Lisa Parsons had sent was old, it was obvious now, maybe even from high school. She'd smiled falsely in the shot, her bangs outdated, her jaw set with forced enthusiasm. Her hands were stacked tentatively, one on the other, like she was worried to touch her own skin. Heidi preferred Lisa Parsons now. She wanted to announce that there existed no handsomer woman, but that might've been awkward. "What do you do in medicine?"

"I'm an orderly." Lisa Parsons rolled her eyes. "Go me."

"I've always dreamed of being an orderly," Heidi said, an appropriate response after someone revealed their profession.

"Oh, honey," Lisa Parsons said. "I'm sure you're smarter than that. I'm just floating until I can afford a tapestry loom. Weaving is my main deal."

Heidi filled with warmth. No one ever called her honey.

"I'm smart too." Kim's voice quivered as though passing through Jell-O. "I get some Bs." Kim yanked strings from a hole in her sweater. They built on her lap like a worm colony.

"Attention, please," announced a lesbian.

"What is it, Anya?" asked Twig Hair, fondling a scone. "Will you sing a ballad?"

Lisa Parsons's hand dropped onto Heidi's knee under the coffee table. Heidi's throat closed. Lisa Parsons stroked her, fanning her hand protectively over Heidi's jeans. Heidi catalogued the weight of each finger, the palm's circle, to re-heat and enjoy later.

The woman named Anya stood up in unlaced boots. She was the only one, besides Lisa Parsons, who wouldn't pass for a lesbian anywhere but here. She had staticky hair and three dimples.

"We indulge Lisa's mentorship efforts," Anya said. "But we never hear from the kids. Sure, we pat their heads and say they're cute and isn't Lisa so great to help, but have you ever thought we're missing an opportunity? These kids must know something we don't about this new 'AOL culture.' After all, these girls materialized from the internet, and to the internet they shall return."

Lisa Parsons squeezed Heidi's knee. "They're kids, you guys. Come on. They're shy."

"Bullshit," said a woman in a moss-colored sweater. "Check out the feisty one." She pointed at Heidi.

All the eyes in the room stuck to Heidi, searing her skin. She wanted to hide in the café bathroom, to breathe in hand soap and digested coffee for as long as it took for their attention to wander, but she couldn't back down now. This was her chance to show Lisa Parsons she was mature, worthy of that hand on her knee, that she wasn't some child, like Kim. Shakily, she clambered onto an aluminum stool. The stool was a mistake, which was clear the instant she mounted it. Now everyone could see the bottoms of her jeans, which she'd stamped all over until she'd shredded the hems.

"Go for it, girl," called a woman with a tiara and a panda purse.

The stool was unsteady and there was nothing to hold on to up there. Lisa Parsons watched with anxious investment, like a mom at a spelling bee. Those fingertips on Heidi's knee, searching. She stood taller, proud. She was doing beautifully. She should pull Kim in.

"Everybody," she said. "That's Kim." Faces turned at once, like satellite dishes, toward Kim. Heidi breathed better with their eyes off her. "You guys say Lisa Parsons helps kids through being gay, but I don't need help. I have Kim." Her voice rolled out, smooth and louder than she'd ever spoken before. "Kim used to live by the ocean, far away from here. There was a Coke factory near her house and Kim has this sea glass that's, like, brown. Kim dated the most popular girl at school, not even in secret. I didn't believe it at first, but it's true. And she had this band? Rainbow Rainbow? Their music made other girls gay." The name of the band, Kim had explained, symbolized two people side by side. The people, who were incidentally both girls, would eventually merge into one rainbow, or girl, but for now were separate ribbons of color, quivering in the lonely sky. "Kim probably helped like five girls realize they were gay with her band." After all, Kim had helped Heidi realize she was gay without an electric guitar or a recorded drumbeat.

These women were decorated and filled out and easy in the world, and then there was Kim, crunched on the couch, her old gray canine exposed. Heidi had told her to get that tooth checked a million times, didn't get why Nancy didn't notice. Against these old, elegant lesbians, Kim was funny-looking and shy. But of course. Heidi's feet went light on the stool, unsteady. She was an idiot. Kim had never dated a popular girl or seduced a teacher. She'd never had a band. She probably hadn't even come out in fourth grade. Heidi had needed to stand up on this stupid stool to figure that out. Her voice flattened: "Kim's neat."

"That's damn right," Anya cried. "This Kim kid's a freaking figurehead."

They turned to Kim with blaring love. Kim eased her feet onto the floor and straightened her back. Her lip twitched. Lesbians beamed at her, and she beamed back. Slowly, so as not to attract attention, Heidi dismounted the stool.

"You're rad," Anya said. "I didn't score a girlfriend until college."

"You're a very impressive young woman, Kim," Lisa Parsons said.

Kim blushed into her shoulder. God, she was endearing. Heidi wanted to bite that sweet smile off her.

"How old were you when you came out?" asked the woman with the panda bag.

Kim showed nine fingers, and the lesbians groaned. Anya shot out of her seat. "That deserves a cappuccino royale."

Kim followed Anya like a dog, without a glance at Heidi. When they were gone, the room tittered back into conversations. But Kim's glow lingered. The women's mouths opened wider, their fingers massaging the air as though it were a sub-stance from which they could pull meaning.

Heidi was abandoned on her end of the room. She pre-tended, like a little kid, that she was invisible with her eyes closed. If Kim was the cool, charming one again, Heidi would rather vanish. But before Heidi enjoyed two minutes of peace, Kim returned, stamping the carpet and carrying on to Anya as though everyone in the room beyond wanted to hear.

Kim rambled on and on about Scituate, speaking stri-dently. So this was her lying voice. Heidi couldn't believe she'd never figured that out before. Kim claimed that the bathrooms in her old middle school were labeled gender-queer, that Gertrude Stein was the centerpiece of each lit course, that the class guinea pigs were lesbians together. Heidi waited for Anya or Twig Hair to scold her. They were adults, they should know better than Heidi, who was too old herself to have believed Kim for so long. Instead, they fell in love with Kim more and more by the second. Any minute, Kim would befriend these lesbians and leave Heidi behind. Heidi's throat swelled and closed.

"Are you okay?" asked Lisa Parsons, padding over. "You look sad."

Lisa Parsons reclaimed her seat on the couch. Under the coffee table, her hand returned to Heidi's thigh, higher than a teacher or a mother or a tutor of wayward youth would dare. The hand slid yet an inch higher. Heidi leaned back against the cushion, nerves glowing from her groin to the tip of her brain. Lisa Parsons plopped her giant handbag on Heidi's lap.

"Hold this," she said, in a voice that was mossy and damp. Before Heidi agreed, Lisa Parsons's hand crossed over Heidi's crotch and dug under the waist of her loose jeans, fingers worming below the elastic of Heidi's underwear, into the cotton crotch, pushing through the few lonely curls of her pubic hair. The feeling was like a tickle but worse, too much, but good. A deep laugh backed up in Heidi's chest.

Across the room, Kim yelped. Lisa Parsons's hand ripped away. Heidi's body seized with panic: she'd been caught. But Kim wasn't watching Heidi and Lisa Parsons. She was only staring at her stupid watch.

"My mom's coming home in twenty minutes."

Heidi barely had time for relief before she was flooded with annoyance. "Since when does your mom care about curfew?"

"We have to go." Kim jumped up.

Heidi longed to push Kim to the floor. Her crotch was still warm and soft from Lisa Parsons's hand, and Heidi needed those fingers back in her underwear, wriggling like slow, gentle worms. Kim could shut up.

"I'll drive you," Lisa Parsons said.

"All the way to the suburbs?" Heidi asked.

The women laughed. Twig Hair made an "ooh" like a ghost. Kim picked up on it, trilled at Heidi, "Ooh, the suburbs." Heidi wanted to scream.

•

At the car, a compact, rickety model with a toy strawberry on the antenna, Lisa Parsons collapsed the front seat and waited for someone to climb in back. Kim didn't move, so Heidi crawled in like a dog, her butt raised in their faces. She swept aside crushed chip bags and CDs so scratched they weren't even shiny.

They drove between lit-up buildings, over the Charles and into Cambridge. Kim and Lisa Parsons chattered about topics Heidi didn't follow, referencing stories they'd swapped in their weeks of IMing. Now that Kim had shed her shyness, she had more to say to Lisa Parsons than Heidi ever would have, all those hours of raw material, intimacies ready to bloom. Lisa Parsons discussed her cat, who Kim called Noodle like he was a personal friend. Lisa Parsons fretted over Nancy's DUI.

"You should tell her how upset you are," Lisa Parsons said. "She thinks you're strong."

Kim picked at the sleeve of her sweatshirt. "I wish I had at least one dad."

Lisa Parsons shook her head with pity. No one included Heidi in the conversation, though she'd spent hours talking through the DUI with Kim, holding her while she cried, arranging rides for Kim when Nancy's license was suspended.

Halfway through Arlington it started to snow, or else it had never stopped in the suburbs. Back at Stony Court, the light was still on in Kim's den. Heidi couldn't bear to sleep on Kim's floor, facing the cigarette butts and the gummy dildo under her bed. If only Lisa Parsons would drop Kim off and pull a U-turn back to the city, fit her hand back inside Heidi's pants.

"Bye," Kim chirped, leaping from the car into a snowbank.

Heidi reached to pull the lever of the seat in front and let herself out. Then she pretended to fumble, wrestling with the front seat like it might attack. Lisa Parsons got up and came around the car. By the time she hunched over to jiggle the passenger seat forward on its tracks, Kim was already way in the distance, halfway across the complex's lawn. She was an idiot to give up this close to the finish line.

Heidi climbed out into the snow, her sneakers immediately soaking through to her socks. Lisa Parsons appeared through the falling flakes, as though she was stuck in a fuzzy TV. "This was fun," she said. If only Lisa Parsons would snatch her and pull her in close.

"Yeah," Lisa Parsons said, peering around. "Is this your apartment?"

"It's Kim's." Heidi tipped her head up so Lisa Parsons could reach her for a kiss.

Lisa Parsons sucked in a breath, her cheeks reddening. When her voice emerged, it squeaked: "I better go."

Before Heidi responded, Lisa Parsons darted back into her car, where she waved manically through the window, face pinched with regret. "Goodbye," she mouthed, the saddest word on earth. Slowly, Heidi turned and stumbled through Kim's tracks. She'd praised Kim so hard, of course the lesbians preferred her. All this was Heidi's own fault. Her shoulders sagged as she walked away.

When Heidi reached the stone with the nameplate of the complex, hands flashed out and caught her ankles. She screamed.

"Shush," Kim said, jerking her behind the stone. Together, they crouched low and sheltered.

The world quieted and became familiar again. Kim's loose mouth and fuzzy hair were the same as they always were, homely but nice, soft and flexible, warmth pulsing off her. The rest of the night unrolled before Heidi: discussing the café under the toxic violet of Kim's black light, a sticky nylon sleeping bag bunched under Heidi's head, their breath mixing and souring the air. They could still have an okay time.

"Keep hidden," Kim said, shuffling over the ice until their knees kissed.

Kim had laughed with the lesbians, head thrown back, shameless. Heidi's cheeks burned. "Why'd you do that?"

"I wanted you to hide with me." Kim giggled, her dead canine popping out. "I didn't mean to scare you. God, you screamed so loud."

"I mean in the café." Heidi straightened her neck. "They liked me and you stole all the attention."

"Who cares? They're a bunch of old people. And you made that whole speech. I thought you wanted them to like me."

She had, at first. She'd pitied Kim.

"I saw your face." Kim brushed snow off her sneakers. "You know I made it up. The band and stuff."

"I've always known," Heidi lied. A darkness opened in her core for lying.

"No." Kim's teeth clicked together in the cold. "I'm glad. You know me, Heidi. I love that." She snatched Heidi's hand.

Heidi waited one polite second before easing her hand free. "That's nice."

"I left my sweatshirt in her car."

"Yeah, right." Kim was meticulous about clothes, especially her purple sweatshirt with 1998 emblazoned across the front. She stored it on a yellow hanger that she swore was made of gold.

"So I'll have to see her again." Kim looked over the top of the boulder. Lisa Parsons's car idled, exhaust integrating with the flakes. Why hadn't she left? Had Kim's trick worked? Was Lisa Parsons gathering the nerve to knock on the condo door and return the sweatshirt?

"Should I go now? I should, right? That's what a date is?" Kim squished her lips like she wanted Heidi to stop her. She inched toward the lot. Heidi caught her by the wrist.

"Don't."

Kim puffed air into her cheeks. "Really?"

Heidi couldn't stand the idea of Kim winning Lisa Parsons over her. "You have all this mystery. The girl with the stories, who doesn't need anyone. You don't want to spoil that, right? I'll get your sweatshirt." She spoke softly. If she sounded kind, maybe she would be. "I'll tell her I've never seen you so happy."

"One practice kiss."

"What?"

Kim pulled Heidi in by the cheeks and slammed their

mouths together so the whole snowy expanse flashed red and throbbing, as though Heidi's head was wrapped in someone's giant vein. Heidi shook free, escaping a licking dog. Soggy and slouched, she deserted the boulder.

Heidi restrained herself from sprinting back to the cozy world contained within the car. She already missed Lisa Parsons's sleek hair, the soft fold of her mouth, the chance to be free of this town with its bowling alleys and cottony dogs and dads who kept you indoors. She stepped up to the car and peered through the passenger window. Lisa Parsons wasn't holding the sweatshirt, awaiting Kim's return. She was slumped over the steering wheel, her hair fanned on the dashboard, like she was dead.

Heidi knocked, loosening the ice shards that had formed on the glass.

Lisa Parsons startled. Shaking her head, recovering, she reached across the empty seat and opened the door.

"Kim left her sweatshirt," Heidi said. The purple heap had been kicked down into the footwell. Heidi was careful not to soil it further as she slid inside.

Lisa Parsons collapsed back against her seat. Her foundation was cut with tear lines. Was this how the internet couple felt before they slipped away: gazing at the soft white world that was about to let them go?

"I can't keep doing this," Lisa Parsons said, her forehead bunched up like a towel. Her voice turned richer. "I've never crossed the line before. You should know that, okay? I get to here and delete my account. I use my name so I won't be tempted. Something's wrong with me."

"Oh." An adult had never spoken to Heidi like this before, in a secret, confidential tone. Heidi wanted to cuddle her spine against the seat and listen forever.

"I don't know if I'd really do it. God, why am I telling you this?" She raked a hand through her hair. "Is Kim okay?"

Heidi nodded, her body floating beyond the car.

"She's not, like, damaged? She seemed off."

"She's fine."

"Okay," Lisa Parsons heaved in a breath. "The stuff I said? It's not, like, traumatizing her?"

Affection for Kim welled in Heidi. "She already knows all that stuff."

Lisa Parsons wiped her forehead with her wrist. "Thanks." She hesitated, staring into her lap. Her voice was so low that it was almost inaudible: "What about you?"

The words surged in Heidi's underwear. She was part of this drama too, battering around at the center of the storm. "I liked when you touched me."

Lisa Parsons snorted, her cheeks flaring red. "You shouldn't."

Heidi couldn't stand it anymore. She leaned across the console and snatched Lisa Parsons's mouth with her own. Lisa Parsons leaned back, and Heidi reached under her shirt, meeting breast abruptly: the slippery fullness, the heavy, taut flesh. The rest of the world blinked out. She'd reached the sweaty center of life: a nipple throbbing on her open palm.

Lisa Parsons pushed Heidi away so hard that Heidi struck the door, which she hadn't fully closed, and it popped open. The air was frozen, a shock. She thrashed as she collapsed into the snow, falling through it deeper than seemed possible, sucking down into the white floor. Any moment Lisa Parsons would dash over, lift her onto the seat, run the heat, and mop her face with Kim's sweatshirt. And there Lisa Parsons was now: reaching over the passenger seat, her eyes beaming like fat stars. She pulled the door shut, and then, shoulders over the wheel, she gunned the engine and was gone.

Heidi didn't have the heart to move. Her arms were wobbly and sore, like she'd swum through custard. Maybe Lisa Parsons had rejected her because she'd sulked in the corner after praising Kim. That had been babyish. She wouldn't kiss herself after behavior like that.

Nancy's silver SUV pulled into the lot. She always parked as far away as possible, to sober up on the walk to the door. Heidi stood up and brushed off snow as Nancy crossed the parking lot and through the complex's front yard with her funny, unmeasured stride. Her hair was down, gray strands swinging. When she reached her building, she leaned against the wall and lit a joint. Heidi walked over and stood beside her. The bricks were ice blocks against her back.

"Taking a stroll, Princess of the Alps?"

Nancy sucked the joint and offered Heidi a drag, the joke of it all over her face. Heidi was Kim's square friend, the kid with the annoying father. But tonight, Heidi accepted. She drew from the clumsy wad of weed and paper, holding in a mouthful of smoke until her eyes watered. So what if Lisa Parsons hadn't worked out? Heidi could do anything. She'd kissed a woman tonight.

A sliver of light shone from the living room above, too steep an angle for Kim to see them. Kim must've been waiting at the computer for Lisa Parsons to get home and IM her, start the relationship for real. Soon Heidi would have to tell Kim that her sweatshirt was gone, that Lisa Parsons wasn't interested, that she was just some pervert, like they should've always known. The good news was, Kim wouldn't mind. They could salvage the sleepover.

"Thanks for having me over," Heidi said.

"You should come around more." Nancy extinguished the joint. "Tell your daddy I'm not so bad."

This was enough, the leftover smoke itching her lungs, hanging out with a grown-up who seemed to care. So it wasn't romantic. So what? She headed for the door.

Nancy pinched Heidi's sleeve, stopping her. "Hey. Heidi. Kim never told you what happened at her old school, did she?" Nancy frowned. "I think you should know."

Nancy was serious. Heidi's limbs tensed. "She told me some stuff."

"Never tell her I told you this. Look. I trust you." Nancy's mouth twitched. "I can trust you, right?"

Heidi's muscles hardened, ready. Maybe someone had posted a picture of Kim's vagina on the school bulletin board or pretended to seduce her and revealed a laughing crowd behind a curtain. Or Kim had been a diminished person in Scituate, maybe: nose aimed at the ground, back curled against not even insults but indifference.

"There was a girl," Nancy said, rubbing her arm. Her chin and mouth were suddenly too soft, drooping. "Kim got the wrong idea. She acts tougher than she is."

Heidi saw it all, in an instant: the girl was tall and long-haired, one shoulder listing to the right, teeth blocky and prominent. The friendship must've closed in until Kim's hand strayed one day to the girl's belly, and then, under her shoulder, to the moist hollow of her armpit. When Heidi pictures Kim and the girl nowadays, she never follows the fantasy to the end: other girls finding out, the best friend ditching Kim, Nancy giving up her own life to move. She holds the story in those early days: the hand, exploring, flesh breathing against fingertips.

Nancy took Heidi's shoulder. "Will you be careful?"

"I'll protect her." She already had, tonight. If it weren't for Heidi, Kim would be in Lisa Parsons's car now, gliding into an unlit drugstore parking lot.

"That's not what I mean. She's fond of you, Heidi."

The ghost pressure of Kim's hands pressed down on Heidi's shoulder, like when they wrestled, holding tighter than Heidi ever held her back. The way Kim watched her glassily when they finished. Kim was at her desk right now, shoulders hunched, the computer open but her focus on the window, waiting not for Lisa Parsons but Heidi.

If only Kim's Scituate was real. The resource room teacher with the futon in the closet, Kelly Stephanie, Rainbow Rainbow. Kim should've stayed in that world forever, where she was safe and popular and happy.

Nancy straightened up. "Be careful how close you get, all right?"

"Yeah." Because hadn't she always known, really?

Nancy wiped her hands on her sweater. "Meet you inside?"

But when Nancy went in, Heidi crossed the yard and the parking lot and headed down Mass Ave. She'd walk the two miles home. She'd give her father a fright no matter how softly she opened the door, but when he saw her, he'd know she was upset. She wouldn't be able to hide her hot cheeks, her busy teeth that had already chewed a cut in her lip. She'd lost Kim, all those adventures and hot dogs and books read together, back-to-back, on Kim's dusty floor. She'd curl in her bed with her quilted pig and muffle the night with heavy blankets. She'd tell herself that leaving was right, that Kim liked her too much, that she'd only get hurt. But in all the lonely years ahead, she'd never be sure if she was just being cruel. As she walked down the street she looked out as far as possible through the night, squinting until the snowflakes were smeared motion on the air.

Boy Jump

THE DAY I WENT TO ZAKRZÓWEK, A BOY DIED. HE'D leaped from the cliff thirty feet above the water. Just as I was leaving my apartment that morning, my landlord told me. I asked whether he meant suicide or for fun. "In Poland it's hard to tell the difference," he said, laughing.

I released my own dry laugh, clutching my backpack strap. I'd only been in the country a few days but I'd already been startled by the blunt expressions, tired eyes, and clenched lips of men shouldering by.

Upon arrival in Krakow I'd been warned of general hazards: pollution, neo-Nazis, the PiS Party, none of which seemed to apply to an afternoon of lake swimming on the outskirts of the city, but you never knew. I would have canceled the outing but it was with Marek, my ticket into Poland, a queer theorist who'd written the recommendation for my postdoc history fellowship. He was insistent on showing me all the city's offerings.

As I passed the muscular monuments of Old Town on my way to cross the Vistula—stallions and saints and a soldier bear—I assured myself: I had to go. Besides, in three days my girlfriend Rosie was due for a visit from Belarus, where she was on a sculpture grant. I was nervous to see her, nervous to tell her about my upcoming changes, which I'd come to Krakow to work out. A dip in a greasy Eastern European waterway could take my mind off her. Even if exposing my curves in a bathing suit was my personal tailored hell.

At Zakrzówek I found Marek waiting for me on a flat expanse of stone cut into the cliff above the water. The entire platform was coated with men collapsed on towels, bellies high and proud, children picking their way between them like survivors among the dead. Marek's barrel chest was out, his round pale head confidently cocked. I asked after the dead boy, worried what had killed him could harm us too.

"Machines are under that water," Marek said, as we advanced into the bodies. At the bushes on the edge of the platform, we passed a wild boar dining from a trash can.

"Is that okay?" I asked.

"Of course not, but what can we do? We can't delete machines. Think of the nonsense!"

"I meant that animal." The boar sported a mohawk of wiry hair down his spine and an aggressively wagging tail. A block of wrapped krówki had lodged in one nostril—I recognized the treat from my landlord's "Hello!" package. The boar was muscular and streamlined, like a hoofed torpedo that could knock us down and consume us with his orange rabbit teeth.

"He is uninvited to this wilderness. Not a natural friend, if you see what I mean. But he will breathe it out as it is only fudge. The machines are there because Zakrzówek was a, what do you call it. Where you dig up rock and pile it for shopping."

"A quarry?" We passed a lounging teen with a braided rattail, sneering at me. I pulled my mask up, disguising the bottom of my face, which was too delicate to pass for male. The top of my face was all right: I had sturdy cheekbones and small eyes, and my new, haphazard haircut—executed with nail scissors on my last night in New Jersey. That was part of why I wore the medical mask. The other reason was that Krakowians lose five years of life to the coal smog that settles in this valley.

"Once upon a time machines pierced this watershed. And the basin filled. All the machines were underneath. They wait still underneath."

At the end of the platform, stone steps led down to the water. UWAGA, a sign beside the steps read, with a cartoon of a screaming, frazzled man, limbs akimbo, tongue out. "Oh no," I said. "We can't swim." Relief sluiced through me, though I'd love Rosie to have heard I'd been killed in a lake of construction equipment. Unlike me, she treasured adventure. If she were here, she would've already clambered into the driver's seat of an underwater bulldozer.

Marek flapped a dismissive hand at the sign and pushed

across the platform between bodies, seeking a spot to claim. Though he was forty-five, round and squat, and I was thirty, I lagged behind. My naked arms burned with shame as he observed me fitting my ass between clots of people. "So the boy landed on machinery?"

"Ha, ha, no!" Marek's lips were dark and wormy, his head too round. "Though many have! This boy was only sixteen. At that age, a boy's heart is not developed. Or it is weak in some fundamental capacity, in terms of very structure. From the hot air to the frigid water, his heart stopped."

Today *was* hot, so hot that the air was white and textured. The quarry unfolded as we crossed the platform: the water shockingly clear, granite cliffs rising on every side, tufted by maples. The cliffs were mirrored in exact, upside-down detail on the surface. Teens shattered the reflections, kicking their legs in freefall, plummeting into the crowd of swimmers as though no one had ever died here. I hadn't imagined Poland contained natural beauty, only slabs of buildings with narrow, deep-set windows. A muscle inside me loosened.

Marek danced between prone bodies, offering cześćs to everyone conscious, until he settled on a slender ribbon of gravel backed up against rockface. "You may remove your mask," he said. "We have achieved leisure."

We spread our towels. Marek removed his T-shirt and hunched on his rectangle of pink terrycloth, spine against the rock, legs generously spread. His positioning left little room for me, consistent with the Polish attitude thus far—the men who didn't stare walked through me like I was vapor. I wedged myself in, leaning against the cliff too, which allowed an inch-wide strip of air between our hips and shoulders, two inches between my legs and the flopped-down spine of the old man beside me. In the water, teens piloted a rubber mattress.

"Well," Marek said. "It's been some time since we've spoken."

Four days had elapsed since our beer in a basement pub in Kazimierz, the old Jewish quarter, where he'd taken me because, alongside polishing my dissertation for publication, I'd professed a desire to study my Jewish roots in the country. The suggestion of my heritage had struck Marek silent, shaking his head, lips working over nothing. I'd squirmed under his scrutiny, hoping that beer would be our sole encounter. Though my grant proposal had bragged about "productive cultural exchange," I'd only chosen Krakow because it was the safest spot near Rosie, but not too near, where I could determine my next steps. She doted on my body and I was afraid that, if I altered anything, she'd bail.

The Polish life of my imagining featured hunching in a concrete café with a pączki and a bad espresso, a blocky proprietor squeezing rags as he loomed behind the counter, me journaling furiously until I decided, yes, I'm going to do this. Yes, I'm going to slide under the knife and fill my body with hormones and change my name to Something and become a boy, honor that earnest impossible childhood wish garbled by a two-decade smorgasbord of female-specific joy and trauma.

If I'd known I'd instead lounge by the water with several dozen naked bodies, ass to ass with a polyamorous, pansexual queer studies scholar, I might've selected Antarctica.

"How have you enjoyed our city?" Marek asked.

"It's fine," I said. "I went shopping." My visit to the corner market had been harrowing. Polish grocery stores foregrounded alcohol and hid the food in a narrow case in back. I'd picked my way through prepared pierogi and butter molded into trees, had purchased buttermilk instead of milk, clotted cream instead of yogurt, false hot dogs instead of real hot dogs. I'd trembled as I claimed my selections, terrified someone would address me in hissy bursts of Polish or bang my head with a pipe for being gay. "I went to the post office." I'd sent a postcard to Rosie in Belarus—I was too scared to visit. Bodies had turned up stabbed at pensions, trans people murdered, pride parades outlawed. Or at least that was my understanding of the situation over the border—I couldn't read about any of it without being sick. The dangers of Poland, in comparison, were manageable. "I can pronounce *do widzenia*."

My shoulder was struck with a hot crack. I lurched forward. Marek had slapped me. My eyes burned—what had I done wrong, so quickly? Was the farewell called by proprietors some hideous swear?

But Marek was chuckling. "You'll be fluent in two minutes," he cried. "In one week!"

His handprint burned sweetly on my spine. I'd never been thumped in a comradely way, by a man. It was nice.

"Now. Why are we waiting?" He leaped up, his shorts rising with him, threatening to reveal more than his creamy thighs. "Don't you have a bathing suit?"

I hadn't removed my T-shirt or sweatpants, didn't relish the idea of stripping down. You'd think, as someone whose toehold in femininity was flimsy enough that a surgical mask converted their gender, I'd be protected from the advances of men, but Marek had one girlfriend and one boyfriend, and I often caught him watching me. I'd recently mail-ordered a queer-friendly bathing suit that promised to suck flat all the lumps of the female form, but only so much could be asked of any fabric.

Marek gazed upon me as I struggled out of my clothes, as did neighboring men. I hurried to undress faster but only got tangled in my pants. I hated removing pants to swim. There was no way to make it not sexual. I did so in a series of queasy jerks, elbows and knees thrust dangerously toward the body beside me, until I was in my boxy black outfit, the dense elastic abusing my breasts so badly that they should have been flatter. I hadn't shaved my bikini line. Marek's eyes lingered on the ragged hairs.

I hustled ahead of him to the stone steps, eager to hide myself in the machine-infested waters. But getting out in front was a mistake: I couldn't track his focus and there was no way to take the jagged staircase briskly. In the water, I relaxed, the freezing gel encasing me, providing a half-transparent privacy. Marek dove in beside me.

All around, skinny arms and legs jostled, heads that had

been shaved until the skin complained with pimples. Bodies dropped from the sky. Wherever I shifted, they followed, as if, out of all the people in this quarry, they were aiming for me. I flinched away from the crowd.

"Marek, cześć," cried a boy, his neck and face dry above the water line, his crown of curls bouncing. He dog-paddled toward us, the skin on his back flexible over muscle, like he had the body of a seal.

"Cześć, Jakub," Marek said, already scanning the water for subsequent friends.

"Hey, you're American," Jakub said when he reached us. His face was rounder and sweeter than anyone's, his flesh elastic. He looked either fifteen or twenty-five. He had a surprisingly sexual quality of movement, so languid in his body that it was as if he controlled it precisely: his own personal flesh robot. I wanted to stroke his springy skin, to pull close to him in the water, to feel against me all that exuberant ease. A pang shot through me for Rosie. She would never guess that I'd consider a man this way. I'd never shared my fascinations. They'd expose too much.

"From New Jersey," I said. How could he tell from just my shoulders and plastered hair? But everyone in the water was absolutely Polish. The features were part of it—broad, pale—but more than that, a certain common toughness or privacy of expression. This was unfair thinking, but it was like if a body landed on them, if they landed on a body, such was life. All tortures had happened here and more lay on the horizon. The air was dense.

"New Jersey," he said. "So exotic, yeah?"

"Very."

"This is our visiting scholar from Princeton." Marek spoke the name of my school as though the royal word was proof Jakub had already messed up. "Ms. Daisy Hoffman."

My cheeks prickled and I ducked below the water before Marek or Jakub read my expression. My name rattled through my head, that lacy, gross flower. Submerged, the cold held me in its dark, lapping green. Marek and Jakub's voices turned bubbly and remote, their bodies dangled, decapitated smears peddling expertly. I longed to hide there until I suffered brain damage.

"Daisy?" Marek called, in his rich voice. "Ms. Daisy?"

I popped to the surface, smoothing down my bangs. "Nice water." I was trembling. How could they stand this icy chill? How could they regard each other with such studied calm, as though under the surface they were completely still?

"Hey, you want a tour?" Jakub bobbed as though on a current.

"Of the city?" I turned to Marek like I required his permission.

"Of Płaszów," the boy said.

"Oh, don't, Kuba," Marek said.

"What is it?" I asked.

"A concentration camp," Jakub said. "Right inside Krakow, though tourists don't know it. From outside it might look much like any city park. Ladies walk their dog and children run over the earth. Scenes that surprise an American. Because of all the dead. You're Jewish?"

"A little." A very little. My Jewish ancestors had abandoned Lesser Poland a century before the war. They'd reached England, where they intermarried with other pasty, moon-faced relatives, posing as Brits for time immemorial. My grandmother never revealed to my father that part of his ethnicity, denied it when my brother chased the genealogy back far enough.

"Wow," Jakub said, bobbing his chin in reverence. "Then I'm sorry, but you really must go."

A man slammed into the water ten feet away. Neither Marek nor Jakub glanced over. Rosie would be excited and horrified by the idea of a death camp park, and I could sweeten her up with my insider knowledge before I had to come clean about me.

"What about the law, though? What do you say on your tour, Kuba? Listen, now." Marek turned to me. "You know this law, yes?"

PiS, the new party in power, had recently deemed it illegal to acknowledge Poland's complicity in the Holocaust. The rule was enforced by an ominous-sounding entity called the Institute of National Remembrance. "Right," I said. But Marek was a queer studies professor. He shouldn't mind some stupid law. None of the Polish historians I'd talked to, here or in America, observed it.

"Oh, Marek," Jakub flung out both hands dismissively, not sinking an inch. "Nothing I say is any problem."

"I'm being tender with our dear visitor." The way Marek spoke to Jakub, eyes narrow, voice thick and breathy, I was certain they'd slept together. Injustice cut through me. I wanted to feel Jakub's soft, powerful shoulders too. And why not me?

"No one will care!" Jakub cried. "You're a pure lunatic."

I laughed in surprise. A body jackknifed into the water over his shoulder.

"Kuba." Marek's face hardened. "Don't." He grabbed my shoulder and pulled me away from Jakub. His grip burned, too firm, brutal. I couldn't handle his touch. I jerked free, my legs sticking out to float. When the water settled, I found that I'd pitched away from Jakub.

"JakubMagik," Jakub called to me, as Marek and I drifted farther away, Marek urging me along with prods to the ribs. "At uj.edu.pl. Two Ks."

"Quiet, you," said Marek, dolphin kicking deeper into the quarry. I followed, though I didn't want to. We reached the center, where the reflection stayed intact whenever we were still, conifers etched in gray on the water's surface. My lungs relaxed—this far out, no one could land on me.

"I won't go," I said, though I'd already committed Jakub's email to memory.

"Go to Płaszów as much as you want. Live and breathe at Płaszów for a hundred years. You think I care about that nonsense law?" Marek pursed his lips. They were still so dark in the water, so it couldn't have been lipstick, but they looked even less natural with the rest of his flesh bleached blue. Maybe they'd been tattooed.

"I said that about PiS because you shouldn't be with Kuba. I'm sorry to tell you, he's a, what do you call it. A person who is like an animal attacking and eating more dainty animals."

"A predator?"

"Yes."

"But he looks like a child."

"That is your first mistake. Jakub is only, perhaps, a child in the heart. He is thirty-seven years old. He may jump at you in attempts to kiss."

In the water, Jakub had felt short. I could push him away easily, his eagerness setting him off-kilter. Rosie would be delighted by my bravery, would think it cheeky I'd kissed a boy. She required more boldness from me and took every chance, even in public, to touch my breasts, my ass, my hips. "I've never had hips in a relationship," she'd said once, squeezing their bulge in Penn Station. "How do you leave them alone?"

As she blushed with arousal, I couldn't bear to tell her that vomit touched my throat and that, when she let me blanket her with my body, my shape disappeared and I became solid and stiff, powerful above her. I itched to even think this, but now that she was far away, life was easier.

"Did Jakub kiss you?" I asked.

As soon as I spoke the words, I regretted it. Marek softened, like his lighting had changed. "I had something with him, yes. Some few months' affair." He pointed his nose at the sky, half of which had been rolled over by clouds. "We made love on occasions. We moved toward a kind of beautiful deep intimacy." He swallowed, neck pulsing. "Alas, but

Jakub had other ideas." Marek's arm popped from the water, shooting droplets as it arced in illustration. "He possessed a region of young men with whom he enjoyed, shall we say, 'passing the time.'"

So Jakub wasn't a predator at all. I wanted to pull his springy body free from Marek's unworthy hands, to change history so they'd never touched. "So he's gay?"

"Ha, ha, certainly."

"So I don't have much to worry about?" I felt a phantom pinch on the back of the neck. Betrayal.

"I mean more that Jakub is not a worthwhile or trusting person for you to spend time with in Krakow. Better yet you stick with me, or historians of repute." Marek gazed off to the cliffs. "Ah. They shuttered the portion where the boy jumped. So cautious!"

I followed his eyes. Young people, mostly boys, catapulted off the rocks that loomed over the water, one after another, so fast that they didn't have time to clear the water for the next jumper. Only a narrow section—about three feet wide—was roped off.

"Let them jump. So they die, so what? People die every year at Zakrzówek. That's practically why they come!" Marek shook his head, spraying quarry water. "Let us go there. Let us cross those stinky ropes and jump from the forbidden spot! Just to show how stupid they are." His chin flushed as though he'd proposed a brave rebellion and couldn't wait even the second it would take for my reaction to register.

This was Rosie's favorite misadventure: dangerous,

pointless, and of zero appeal. The very attitude that won her fellowships: her sculptures were formed from live bees, aspic, lead, Freon, a paste made from simmered poison ivy. She measured hydrochloric acid in flimsy plastic water bottles, harvested cyanide from apple seeds, dusted fairground butter sculptures with lye. Everyone worshipped her daring. Such a little girl with so much mercury. No one saw her as I did, in sweatpants, scarfing pudding over the sink, worrying her work was all carnival.

Straight from a marriage, Rosie had attacked me with her latent lesbianism, molding my contours with strong hands, building up my shape. Even her misguided attention was narcotic. I always said yes. We'd attempted to spend the night on the observation deck of the Empire State Building and were kicked out only when she spray-painted the security cameras. We'd swum in the East River, ducking from barges and ferries. We'd devoured full platters of Princeton's half-baked, pockmarked cafeteria pizza, its beige cheese as toxic as any of her sculptures.

My cowardice about changing my body would only disgust her. If I jumped from the cliff, I'd at least have a story about my courage. But the idea of falling, my body loose in the open air, clenched my intestines. "No."

Marek regarded me with disgust. He plowed his mushroom body back to shore.

•

My tour with Jakub was several hours before Rosie's arrival. I rented a heavy, battered city bike for the ride, chipped blue paint and egregiously chunky. When I biked up a hill— thankfully, there weren't many—it was like heaving the steel frame on my back. To distract myself, I scrolled through Rosie's recent texts: *Eat that Polish butter hard, sweetcakes; Damn those dumplings look like your ass; Need you here so bad.* Frumpy bald walkers overtook me on both sides.

Jakub was already waiting. He was thicker today in his red puffer jacket. All shiny and flexible, he jiggled on his heels. What would I do with that much energy? I'd savor every second. "You've come! Beautiful. Welcome to Płaszów."

I ripped off my mask, ashamed for him to think I disparaged the air of his country, even though, under the cotton, my chin and upper lip already sprouted sweat-induced blackheads. He was right about the camp: green fields stretched in every direction, pedestrians leashed to standardly unfriendly Polish dogs, bikes bumping over grass, old couples dressed as though for a living history museum, promenading in silence, the men a few steps ahead. Sun touched every example of Saturday afternoon Polish stoicism. Jakub took off at a clip.

"There's the Gray House," he said, pointing to an institutional building, the hue of dirty snow. "Prisoners were tortured in that basement. These weeds used to be a fire-prevention pond. Allianz made camps like this one dig them to meet insurance standards." He let the statement hang over the bank of phragmites. The name of the modern insurance agency was so wrong in the context of the Holocaust. I touched the fragile stem of a weed, which felt like any plant.

"Life expectancy was three months for those digging the ponds," said Jakub. "All filled in now. Be mindful of some certain holes. Ah, here's one. Remnant of the sewage system. And there, the latrine." He indicated a dent in the grass. "Orphans hid here when the children and elderly were killed, come along!" He threw his hands above his head and flitted away. I hesitated at the hole, picturing the cliff jumper crammed down there, all baby face and immature heart.

"Can you imagine these fields of bunkhouses? People made brushes here! Everyone had to make a certain number of brushes per day. A lot of brushes, I know, I don't have the number, but picture, please, if you will, some entire mound of brushes. Even a young boy had to make brushes, like thirteen years of age. And one day a particular boy couldn't make enough brushes, and an old man made his brushes for him—can you imagine? Only in a place of death and horror, only in a time of entire deprivation, can Poles come together to help make brushes."

"That's too bad." I'd never been on such a jaunty Holocaust tour.

"No. Americans are worse!" He slapped my shoulder, sending shivers through me, before halting at a sinewy cross decorated with a crown of thorns and a tiny Jesus. "Now this is just too much a pity."

I stared for a long time before I understood what was wrong. The monument was generic, familiar, found in miniature in any Queens front yard. But then I realized—of course.

He shook his head. "And look what they wrote."

The placard at the base of the monument was dedicated to "Poles," with no mention of Jews, and doomed the dead to lie under a sinister Christian blaze of "perpetual light."

I longed to go home, to lie down, and steel myself for Rosie's arrival. My lunch was a roiling mush inside me. So many doughy pierogi, a brown rainbow of fillings: sweet cheese, lentils, fistfuls of meat. So many salty vegetarian hot dogs, enjoyed cold from the pouch.

"Disgusting, right?" Jakub said. "There's a monument in here for the Jews, at least. Through there." He flapped a hand at some trees. "But even so. Think of the others. There's no monument in all Krakow, for example, to gays." He looked at me pointedly. "There's never any monument of gays, is there, Daisy?"

"I'm sure there are plenty," I muttered, hoping he'd hurry past this revelation. If he thought I was a lesbian, he'd never touch me.

Jakub shook his curls and bounded across the park to the next point of interest: a hulking Communist monument, granite hacked brutally into the shape of bowing prisoners with a gash through their torsos. "You see this?" Jakub pointed out the inscription. *To the memory of the martyrs murdered by the Nazi perpetrators of genocide in the years 1943–45.*

"Martyrs volunteer," I said.

"The Poles don't come to this conclusion, but you are American. And Jewish, right?"

"Sort of. A little."

"I love Jewish people."

"Are you Jewish?"

He set a hand on his throat. "I must tell you, I feel Jewish so deeply in my heart. You know, Poland was once a diverse country. You don't believe it, but we had many ethnic minorities—Ruthenians, Lithuanians, Jews, Ukrainians, Belarusians—all living together so happily."

I'd heard this argument before, from defensive Polish historians. "But things sort of changed, right?" I couldn't help it. The populations he'd mentioned had been banished with border redraws, exiled, slaughtered, and burned.

His eyes narrowed, his mouth molding into that routine Polish frown. "Well, I suppose I can't fight against you. But by now we certainly embrace Judaism. Haven't you seen the restaurants in Kazimierz? The Jewish Culture Festival?"

There was a row of restaurants in the Jewish quarter, hung with traditional caricatured portraits of hook-nosed misers clutching coins, believed to attract money to a household. The restaurants claimed to be kosher but were run by gentiles. The Jewish Culture Festival, according to my advisor, though bravely founded during Communism, was presided over by a Polish gentile who spoke with a false Yiddish accent. "Don't you find that stuff a bit, like, disturbing?" I asked. "Like, fetishizing?"

"What do you mean?" He stopped hard in the grass, the lovely mechanism of his body stilling all at once. "It's very nice to like Jews, and to support Jews, and to bring across the Jewish culture. Don't you appreciate it?"

"Well, I'm not really Jewish." I shifted my shoulders as though redistributing the burden of the sunshine.

He huffed a breath. "So silly! If people care about your culture, that's a perk! Here I am, every day, giving tours of this park. You'd never have known it was anything if it weren't for a man like me."

The light fell across his collarbone, where his puffy coat had slipped open. The skin was so vulnerable there, pulsing.

We settled cross-legged at the base of the monument, which obstructed it for visitors. Except there were no visitors. The monument faced a street dominated by a blocky, mysterious complex with the ominous name of Castorama. A few sad candles lay scattered at the monument's foot. Pinching blades of grass from the earth, Jakub explained that houses and businesses had been built on top of the concentration camp, whose territory stretched beyond the limits of the park.

"That's amazing you're Jewish." His curls fell loose across his forehead. I had to look away, he was too eager and sweet.

"Marek said I shouldn't meet you," I said.

Jakub's face hardened. Maybe now he'd force a kiss. But, quickly enough, he relaxed back into puppyish cheer. "I know it."

"He said you two had a romance."

Jakub laughed. "Oh, Marek. Unrepentant liar."

"Really? He lied?"

"Of course. Look at his head!"

We giggled together, a rushing release. Poor sturdy, egg-headed Marek. Surely not Jakub's type at all.

"We did fuck of course," said Jakub.

I stopped laughing. Jakub had bought into all that cheap swagger, so easy and unearned?

"I thought we might go somewhere." He waved his hand. "But later, he wasn't interested." His voice thickened. "Alas. All is well."

Maybe Jakub had been younger when the two of them fucked, his youth rendering him as big-eyed and helpless as me: new and anxious in a foreign country. Marek got off on touring a wide-eyed kid around. Now that Jakub was muscular under his baby fat, Marek had lost his ability to wow. "His loss," I said.

Jakub curled his lip. "But we're off track." Calmer now, a surefooted historian, he asked if I remembered the bumpy lawn beside the cross.

"Not really." Wasn't this whole place one bumpy lawn?

"Do you want to know? It's ghastly."

I wanted to know.

Jakub explained that the lumps were a group burial ground in an old Austro-Hungarian rampart nicknamed by the prisoners Hujowa Górka, a pun on Dick Hill. The site before us, at the base of the martyrs' monument, was another burial site, established later, when the Dick filled to the brim with bodies. The new site, a basin below the sculpture, was called Cipowy Dołek, meaning Pussy Hole. He pointed to each of our crotches to press his point. He looked at me, eyes sparkling. "Funny, yeah?"

I set my shoulders back, straining to watch him with the steady gaze of a man accustomed to concentration camp dick jokes. I placed my bike helmet over my lap so he couldn't further reference my anatomy.

"But you aren't a girl, are you?" He reached over, diddled a finger of hair I hadn't cut short enough.

"What?" I said, startled. "You mean, like, a woman?" I skipped on the blobbiness of the word.

He touched the back of my neck. His stroke was firm and clinical, like he didn't have to bother considering how I'd receive it, his gaze assessing my mullet and my hoodie dragged low over my hips, my snug fashion sweatpants, the mask around my neck still blocking the fine tip of my chin. There was nothing erotic in his painful, dragging strokes. "No," he said, drawing out the word, like I was an idiot. "Daisy. But you're a guy, actually. Right?"

I pressed myself more solidly into the grass. I shook my head.

A smug smile spread over his face. "Ah ha. But, I see, you don't get it yet. But soon."

"I do get it." My voice was a whine, like a kid. "So shut up."

He laughed. "I knew by the way Marek ushers you all over. He never does that with a girl."

"That's ridiculous," I said. "Marek has a girlfriend." I was trembling. Jakub could tell I was trans? How? Though it was all I wanted, it was like he was staring through to my organs and judging their spots.

"Only to keep the boyfriend. He likes a straight boy, and you, my friend, are straight."

My throat clumped into knots. How awful to be suddenly accused of heterosexuality, even if it was true. My voice creaked: "What gave it away?"

He leaned his head back, his mouth opening in a silent laugh. "Oh, I know a straight when I see a straight."

A straight white man—that was my future. Trundling around pretending to be Jewish to steal a bit of pseudo-minority status. I'd turn invisible, privileged, easy in the world. Who would I be when I wasn't exactly me anymore? Nothing like Jakub. A whiney, diminished man, disavowing the privilege I obviously hoarded, and worse, that I'd bought for myself.

Rosie had left her tattooed, compact husband for me, considering our love her next great, dangerous adventure. She wouldn't be able to bear the new me, and I couldn't either. All my nebbish anxiety was only endearing in a girl. Jakub was still giggling, hand sealing his mouth. I vibrated with desire, but rage threaded through it. I wanted to kick him in the stomach, to shut him up for acting like he knew more about me than I did. The feeling swelled: urgent, muscular. I wanted to fuck him, hard, to peel off his body and wrap myself in it.

I lunged out, meaning to touch his thigh, even kiss him, but the heel of my hand grazed his balls, shockingly loose and soft in his silky athletic pants.

"Hey," he said, his color turning ashen. He sliced his hand through the air as though his English had deserted him. "No, no."

"I'm sorry." I jumped back. He was way overreacting. "I didn't mean to."

Jakub kept slicing his hands, curls dancing, as if I'd physically harmed him. Why was he freaking out? People had died on this grass. Dogs had shit and children had scampered over ground where people had lined up for head counts. Even looking that misery in the eye was invasive, even considering their trauma at all. But that was my job: poring over the hardships of others and pretending to understand. I stood up in three separate creaky motions. "I'm getting out of here."

"No," he said. "It's fine. I'm fine." His voice was a whisper. All the menace of his sturdy Polish face distilled to soft, rodenty worry. I looked away. "It's just—never mind." His voice shook like he feared what he might tell me. "Forget it. Let's keep up with the tour."

"No," I said, so forcefully that he shrank into the lee of the monument. He looked like me: hunched, defensive. I left him there, shaking his head. I couldn't even bear to say goodbye.

•

Late that evening, when the sun was gold and thick on the cliff face, I returned to Zakrzówek. I was still in the parking lot when my phone sounded a cool blip like a raindrop. On the screen was a text from Jakub: a crying emoji, the blue of sorrow draining down through yellow flesh. *I hope you can understand I've been touched this way too much, and I don't take it anymore.* The breath died in my throat. Had closeted Poles been rough with him, half-hating him even as they fucked? Even Marek hadn't been kind. How was I better? Closeted too, leaping at him like a wolf. My mouth soured. And next, a text from Rosie: *Landed early. Come get it, girl.* I stared at the phone way too long, the day dimming around me. Then I tucked it into my pocket.

Even though the sun frosted the leaves such a rich yellow, even though it was warmer than earlier, the stone platform over the quarry was all but deserted. On the cliff, no one jumped. There were overlapping youths, asleep in street clothes. Rosie was in the dinky airport, checking her phone: impatient, horny, worried. Let her wait.

I found the section roped off for the boy. How had they pinpointed where he left earth? I stripped down to my swimsuit, the grass slimy on my bare feet. Jakub had swum through this water, between falling bodies and angry Polish teens, in a country that had outlawed abortion, forced out almost half of the Supreme Court, and allowed towns to establish themselves as LGBT-Free; he'd flashed his body, flirting openly with Marek, still so impossibly sweet. I lived across a river from Manhattan, and I was afraid to make a single move toward transitioning. Rosie loved me, and she loved adventure. There was a chance, if slim, she'd still want me. I lined up my toes with the edge of the cliff.

Thirty feet was not so much from above. Water looks like water from any height. The muscles in my legs twitched to jump, but I held myself solidly to the earth, squinting across the ripples to the array of tidy man-cut cliffs.

Below the surface, all that granite had been scraped out before the flood. Where was it now? In bathrooms in America, black and veiny and chic? In the dicks of horse sculptures, because monument horses were always male? In trinkets squeezed by anxious children? It didn't matter. All of it was gone now, carted far away from here.

A ding sounded into the canyon, ringing against the basin, and I turned, expecting the boar, or Jakub, seeing through me again, but the sound broadcast from my pocket. Another emoji, this one with downcast eyes, like a chastised child. I couldn't bear Jakub, crouched on the camp lawn or in a Communist block apartment somewhere, communicating with cartoon circles. I was a monster. Another ping, Rosie: *Where are you?* Electricity rioted in my core. Soon she'd meet me with my haircut, my Polish hoodie, and my news. Whichever way her expression shifted at what I had to tell her, I was going forward. Even if that meant facing every step alone and heartbroken.

I'm not ready, I typed. When I hit send, my mask loosened

and slid free, dangling around my neck. The wind cooled the pads of my cheeks. I knew what I was doing, and that was enough, for now. Soon I'd be immersed in the water, cold and deep and heavy.

Acknowledgments

Thank you so much to my brilliant and visionary agent Samantha Shea for standing by me through the years and for her radical, creative solutions, and my genius of an editor Leigh Newman, who sees through my tricks and makes everything a thousand times better with her keen eye and breathtaking imagination. I could never ask for better supporters than the two of you. Thank you to Kaiya Shang at Scribner UK for finding me across the ocean and believing in me, and to Valerie Borchardt and everyone at Abner Stein for making it happen. Thank you also to Cassie Gross, Rachel Ludwig, and everyone else at Georges Borchardt Literary Agency. Thanks to Alisha Gorder, Wah-Ming Chang, Sue Ducharme, Megan Fishmann, Nicole Caputo, Rachel Fershleiser, Katie Boland, and everyone at Catapult. What a perfect home—I'm so lucky.

Thank you to the magazine editors who took chances on the stories in this book and made them so much better: Emily Nemens at *The Paris Review* and *The Southern Review*; Hasan Altaf at *The Paris Review*; Cara Blue Adams for accepting "Pioneer" initially, years before I met her; Mark

Drew at *The Gettysburg Review*; Will Allison and Patrick Ryan at *One Story*; and Adeena Reitberger and Rebecca Markovits at *American Short Fiction*. Infinite thanks to Bill Henderson at Pushcart Press, who gave me my first break and made a home for three of my stories, whom I've never had the privilege of meeting in person, and who must be a saint among humans.

Thank you to all of the intrepid civilians who read these stories in various forms and made them what they are, many of them dear friends I rely on deeply: Jamel Brinkley, Devyn Defoe, Neha Chaudhary-Kamdar, Gothataone Moeng, Sterling HolyWhiteMountain, Georgina Beaty, Nicole Caplain Kelly, Evgeniya Dame, Asiya Gaildon, Jamil Kochai, Adam Johnson, Judith Claire Mitchell, Jesse Lee Kercheval, Ron Kuka, Allie Rowbottom, Sarah McColl, Kimberly King Parsons, Mary South, Jean Garnett, Lydia Fitzpatrick, Marian Palaia, Andrew Mortazavi, Yuko Sakata, Janice Shapiro, Hannah Oberman-Breindel, Olga Zilberbourg, Greg Hunt, Jenn Salcido, Grainger David, Kyle McCarthy, Kai Carlson-Wee, Jacques Rancourt, Josh Kalscheur, Zinzi Clemmons, Leigh Feldman, Michelle Wildgen, Maud Casey, and Lan Samantha Chang, especially, for pushing me toward the light with "Laramie Time." And thanks to Alexander Lumans for reading the whole manuscript, in different form, some years back.

For late-stage specialized reads and research help (not to mention emphatic and undeserved cheerleading), thank you so much to Adam Schorin, Jessamine Chan, and Matt

Wood, three dear friends I am so lucky to have lending their thoughts and attention and support to this process.

Thank you for the time and space and, most importantly, faith in me: Yaddo, Hedgebrook, the Bread Loaf Writers' Conference, Djerassi, Lighthouse Works, Millay, Jentel, the Virginia Center for the Creative Arts, StoryKnife, the James Merrill House, Brush Creek, the Sitka Center for Art and Ecology, the Vermont Studio Center, Caldera, the Santa Fe Art Institute, and Grace Paley Palooza. And thanks especially to MacDowell, where I started and finished this book, ten years apart. Thank you so much to Diana and Jim Lett, Sarah LaBrie and Justin Lerner, Carmiel Banasky, Raky Sastri and Laurelin Kruse, and Sophia Cosmadopoulos for lending me your lovely homes while I worked on this book.

Thank you for the gift of money and time, without which I certainly would've been knocked off this path years ago: the Fulbright Commission, the Rona Jaffe Foundation, the Stegner Fellowship Program, the Elizabeth George Foundation, and Princeton University. Your generosity made this possible.

Thank you so much to my colleagues and students at the University of Wisconsin-Madison, the University of Michigan, Emory University, the Young Writers Workshop, and Stanford University—what an inspiration and privilege to know you.

Thank you to my mentors. I can't believe I've had the fortune to receive the wisdom of such luminaries through the years: Lynda Barry, Lorrie Moore, Elizabeth Tallent, Steven Bogart, Peter Ho Davies, Jane Hamilton, the late Michael Fiveash, Connie Lane, and Anne Sanderson.

Most queers couldn't survive a minute without friends—
and I am an especially hopeless case. To those wonders not
otherwise mentioned who provided crucial support during
the process of writing this book: Wilder Allison, the late John
Allen, Margaret Allen, Ari Banias, Elissa Bassist, Nicholas
Boggs, Greg Brown, Michelle Chan Brown, Julie Buntin,
Casey Cep, Serena Chopra, Jennifer duBois, Emma Eisen-
berg, Genevieve Frisch, Sarah Frisch, Phoebe Gloeckner,
Jeremy Hamilton, Henry Hoke, Allegra Hyde, Becky James,
Tennessee Jones, Reese Kwon, Gabriella Levine, Karan
Mahajan, Sallie Merkel, Nina McConigley, Coco Moseley,
Nicole Salazar, sam sax, Michael Sears, Vaughn Shinall, Jay
Sibara, Susan Steinberg, Barrett Swanson, Riley Wise, and
everyone I missed, which is probably another dozen people.

Special thanks especially to the extra special people who
tolerated and supported and loved me in the darkest moments of the journey of these stories, my perfect cohort—
Fatima Kola, Brendan Bowles, Kate Folk, and Matthew
Denton-Edmundson—for making my work so much better, for caring for me, for so many hikes and picnics and
bonfires and so few hugs, restaurants, and dance parties.
I'm so grateful we ended up together. Melissa Febos, Claire
Vaye Watkins, Braden Marks, LuLing Osofsky, Becca
Albee, and Josie Sigler for answering my communiques instantly and lovingly and talking me through the hardest
parts; Maud Streep, Francesca Mari, and Miranda Feather-
stone for being my first and oldest writing friends; Yelena
Akhtiorskaya, for wild swims and thunderstorms; Michelle

Chun, for Brandon and Leopold, assorted dogs, and "writing group"; Aurora Masum-Javed, from Iliamna to the Porcupines; Margaret Ross, preplague South Bay copilot and "best friend from college," for indulging hours of my walk-writing and letting me see things from time to time through the filter of your brilliant mind; Kirstin Valdez Quade for reading everything I wrote for almost a decade and being by my side for a quarter of my life on numerous continents; Julie Rossman, Josh Arnoudse, Raky Sastri, Olivia Verdugo, Elisabeth Halliday-Quan, Duncan Riddell, and Gwen Tulin for between twenty-four and thirty-six years of friendship apiece but especially, in this case, veronique d'entremont for squeezing pus and blood from pumps embedded in my body; Emily Ray Reese (and Leonard and Frida) for treks and laughter; Ali Shapiro, for wolf fur and overtime; Sarah LaBrie for doughnuts and sharing work; Young Jean Lee for walks at dawn in sorrow.

And thank you, lastly, to my family of origin for their years of support and love, especially Marion Belcher and Sandy, Evy, and Lola Anton; my parents, John and Sarah, and my siblings, Chris, Annie, and Gillian. Thank you for letting me follow this bleak and restless path. And, lastly, thanks to my niblings: Jonah, Remy, Jacob, Cole, and Eden. I feel better about the future when I think of you five out there being weird for the rest of us.

Sending all of you back love that will never be enough.

© Emily Ray Reese

LYDIA CONKLIN has received a Stegner Fellowship, a Rona Jaffe Foundation Writers' Award, three Pushcart Prizes, a Creative Writing Fulbright in Poland, a grant from the Elizabeth George Foundation, scholarships from Bread Loaf, and fellowships from Emory, MacDowell, Yaddo, Hedgebrook, Djerassi, and elsewhere. Their fiction has appeared in *Tin House*, *American Short Fiction*, and *The Paris Review*. They've drawn comics for *The New Yorker*, *The Believer*, *Lenny Letter*, and other publications. They are currently the Helen Zell Visiting Professor in Fiction at the University of Michigan.